BOTHELFORD'S GONE

BOTHELFORD'S GONE

Edward McLaren

The Maldon
Press

Copyright © 2026 The Maldon Press
The Maldon Press is an imprint of Redoubt Press, LLC

The Maldon Press
P.O. Box 508
Blowing Rock, NC 28605
www.vaubanbooks.com

Library of Congress Control Number 2026932158

ISBN 979-8-9938908-0-7 (paperback)

Front cover illustration, Mélibée by Francis Picabia
Back cover photograph, Oxford Street in Rotherham by Martin Speck
Design and composition by Robert Kern, TIPS Publishing Services,
Carrboro, NC

1 2 3 4 5 6   30 29 28 27 26

PREFACE

In 1948, as Prime Minister, Clement Attlee passed the British Nationality Act to redefine British nationality to refer to citizens of 'the United Kingdom and the Colonies'. This gave citizens of Pakistan and India, which had become independent in 1947, the right to move to Great Britain, to vote, and to work. They took their customs with them.

Almost immediately, British newspapers began to share reports of Muslim grooming gangs in Bradford, Kent, West Yorkshire, Lancashire, Hartlepool, Faversham, Nelson, Halifax, Oldham, and London. After seventy years, the Independent Inquiry into Child Sexual Abuse, released in 2022, studied the emergence of an organised Muslim rape culture in Britain and noted the culture's tremendous growth in the 1970s. This was a period characterised by increased immigration from Southeast Asia and Africa, as well as the beginning of the suppression of freedom of speech under Solicitor General Frank Soskice's Race Relations Act of 1965. Observing America's struggle with segregation and racism, the British state moved fast to punish vocal political opposition to immigration. The British government also began to punish discussion of the rape gangs.

As anti-discrimination legislation expanded and the culture of groomers thrived and grew under the protective wing of the State and top-down multiculturalism, the gangs consolidated power more easily than ever before. In 2025, seventy-five years after the first gang rapes, the Casey Audit, written as a follow-up to the Independent Inquiry, reported 'many examples of organisations avoiding the topic altogether for fear of appearing racist, raising community tensions or causing community cohesion problems.' According to the Casey Audit, 'In Rotherham, Operation Stovewood found that nearly two-thirds of suspects—64 per cent—were recorded as having a Pakistani background, even though Pakistanis make up just about 4 per cent of the town's population. By contrast, just 22 per cent of the suspects are recorded as British.' This meant that one in eight Pakistani men in Rotherham had raped an English girl at the time.

As for the number of victims, the report noted, 'No one knows the true scale of child sexual exploitation (CSE) in Rotherham over the years. Our conservative estimate is that approximately 1400 children were sexually exploited over the full Inquiry period, from 1997 to 2013.' In 2015, the Labour MP for Rotherham, Sarah Champion, told *The Mirror*, 'There are hundreds of thousands and I think there could be up to a million victims of exploitation nationwide.' She was extrapolating figures from Rotherham nationally. The Casey Audit indicated that in at least two-thirds of child sexual exploitation cases, the ethnicity of perpetrators was deliberately not recorded. The police prioritized their fear of ethnic tension over recording the facts of the abuse of the girls.

In the testimony of both victims and perpetrators, a common theme emerges: a hatred of victims for their ethnicity as white British natives and as young non-Muslim women; one of the victims from Dewsbury was told by her rapist, 'We're here to fuck all the white girls and fuck the government.' We now know that survivors were also subject to child sexual abuse by Rotherham police. When girls went to the police, some were raped again or sent back to the gangs. Often, the girls were drugged or made to drink, and the police excused what happened to them as the result of their poor decision-making as 'child prostitutes'.

In 2018, the Conservative Home Secretary Sajid Javid, who has Pakistani heritage and was born in Rochdale, wrote a letter to prevent the deportation of the ringleaders of the Rochdale Muslim rape gang; the Home Secretary had 'decided not to make a deprivation order in respect of you'. Then, in 2022, Javid responded to a tweet by Nigel Farage, which concerned figures from the Office of National Statistics showing that London, Manchester, and Birmingham had all become minority white cities, by saying, 'So what?'

Despite promising to 'Get Brexit Done', Boris Johnson's time as Prime Minister is defined more than anything else by the 'Boriswave', during which migration increased from 737,000 in 2021 to over 1 million in 2022 and 1.3 million in 2023. In 2024, immigration was down to 948,000, with

EU nationals making up only 19 per cent of total immigration, in contrast to non-EU nationals making up 81 per cent (766,000). These non-EU nationals came predominantly from India, Pakistan, and Nigeria. According to the World Population Review, Great Britain had 73,590 cases of rape in 2022, making it the rape capital of Europe; the ONS recorded 71,227 cases in 2024. This is in contrast to the 12,295 cases recorded by the ONS in 2002: Britain's rate of rape has increased sixfold.

In February 2022, Johnson's Conservative government was responsible for a massive accidental data leak of the information of Afghan fighters during the US withdrawal from Afghanistan. A super-injunction was passed that would prevent the press from speaking about the potential immigration of up to 750,000 Afghan fighters over the next two years. This was leaked during Keir Starmer's government when an ex-fighter from Afghanistan attempted to blackmail them.

In 2024, Labour MP Naz Shah reposted and liked a tweet saying, 'Exactly Areeq, those abused girls in Rotherham and elsewhere just need to shut their mouths. For the good of #diversity!' The same year, a man named Derek Heggie was sentenced to a year in prison for making 'grossly offensive' comments on YouTube videos, such as stating that 'young white girls are being raped by these grooming gangs that worship the Prophet Muhammad.' Another man, David Jordan, was sentenced to over two years behind bars for shouting 'fucking paedos' during a protest outside a hotel housing migrants and because he told the police to 'fuck off'. Meanwhile, Peter Lynch was condemned to spend two years and eight months behind bars because he 'waved conspiracy theory placards' and 'screamed abuse at police' outside a Rotherham asylum hotel. Lynch shouted at officers, 'You are protecting people who are killing our kids and raping them.' He was a grand-father; he killed himself in prison. In contrast, Abdul Rauf, a member of a grooming gang, was sentenced to six years in prison for trafficking and conspiracy; according to the judge, there were between ten and twenty occasions when he drove a fifteen-year-old girl in his taxi to a flat, where he and other men 'had sex' with her. He served only two and a half years of his sentence and has not been deported from Britain. As of now, he remains free.

In 2025, Professor Matt Goodwin reported that white Brit-ish people will be a minority in their own country by 2063, with the most fertile population in modern Britain being Pakistani Muslims (total fertility rate: 2.95), followed closely by Nigerians.

On 25 August 2025, the Centre for Migration Control recorded a 'surge in migrant crime between 2021 and 2024', including a '62% increase in sexual offence convictions', a '77% increase in theft convictions', a '19% increase in robbery con-victions', and a '105% increase in criminal damage convictions.'

Everything in this book is based on documented past events. This is a true story for the future.

If man could see
  The perils and diseases that he elbows,
  Each day he walks a mile; which catch at him,
  Which fall behind and graze him as he passes;
  Then would he know that Life's a single pilgrim,
  Fighting unarmed amongst a thousand soldiers.
  It is this infinite invisible
  Which we must learn to know, and yet to scorn,
  And, from the scorn of that, regard the world
  As from the edge of a far star.

—Thomas Lovell Beddoes, 1850

ONE

It was the kind of place where something dearly wished to happen but never could. Patience had left the town, even though its pain of waiting for tourists, its grief at having its parks unused, its loneliness of having its high street gradually deserted had not. If the town could dream, it dreamed desperately, and its scarred, potholed roads, whether Roman or Victorian originally, appeared to lie in anticipation of a sterner kind of people than those who drove blithely over them then.

But what was it that the town wanted? Perhaps it looked upon its denizens as a disappointed ancient ghost, who, having nourished their ancestors with her woods, her coal reserves, her fish and rivers, her corn and flour, found out too late that all this effort had simply been to accomplish the generation of idiots before her. In comparison to the brisk miners, the able goldsmiths, the riotous bawds, the hilarious warriors, the able foresters, and the feeling and unopinionated intellectuals of previous ages, there was nothing particularly of note about the young people of the town in those days, except that a few of them cared extremely about politics and not one had any more interest than their parents in local affairs if they did not directly concern them. In another age, a scribe might have written or a bard might have sung that the people of Bothelford worried for others as a vain man worries for a reflection of himself. But since those ages had long passed away, nobody said anything, or nothing worth remembering anyway. In a pub, perhaps, a young man would feel out an idea and try to express it to another, his intellectual mentor, and a thought would emerge organically as of old. Yet never would it concern itself with Bothelford, with the destiny of the town, but always with an infinite number of trifling foreign affairs. Or they would talk of money, of men and women—of men and women as general *concepts*, whilst the speakers met neither at all regularly.

In Bothelford, conversation, even good conversation, was like trying to paint faces onto ghosts. Whatever hauntings had gone on previously in St Michael's church (and there had been plenty), which sat at the centre of the town, were hardly as disturbing as the spectres that most people had become to each other. In fact, the visit of Marine Emery—a phantom apparently alluded to by the Venerable Bede, although that is just hearsay—was noted in the folklore of the town as a great positive. Not so with the population of the living. Marine Emery would bless those who came to St Michael's on the ninth of September, once every three years. This numerical significance—of nine-nine-three—was disputed by the few very, very old people who remained in the town. Some held, as former generations had informed them, that nine-nine-three referred to the number of wings, arms, and faces of a specific angel, perhaps even St Michael himself. Yet when asked how this calculation had been made, most would be unable to answer. 'That is how the story went ...' was what they'd usually say.

Marine Emery, who manifested with a red halo behind her head, was not prepared to answer in more detail. All she would do, according to the ninety-three-year-olds who remembered her, was walk down the aisle of St Michael's, bearing a kind of hollow candle that was made of dust, and fade into the woods at the exit. Reportedly, her face had no eyebrows. Her eyes were a bright, yet somehow sorrowful, reptilian green. She would be wearing a long, white, floor-length gown. Under her breath, she would say the phrase: '*I knoo what it 'tis tha happens ...*' in a strong regional dialect, but nothing more. It was a kind of ghostly nonsense speak, unlike the all-too-accurate, all-too-discerning talk amongst the people of Bothelford.

Oddly enough, however, those dead and gradually dying people familiar with Marine Emery, or just her story, uniformly agreed that her one nonsense phrase referred to something coming, rather than something that had occurred in the past when she was alive. Given that when someone encountered Marine Emery at St Michael's, they were always rewarded with tremendous luck—winning the lottery, in one recorded case, and getting married in another—the elders generally assumed that whatever 'happening' she mentioned in her refrain would be of the same nature. To them, she was a local goddess of mercy. To young people, whether fifty or forty, whether thirty or ten, she was not anything. She was the muttering of crazy old fogies whose prejudices were as primitive as the soil and as worthy of neglect. Even more so was the 'elf', the wayfarer who, the most ridiculous of the ridiculous said, prophesied her coming, wearing a shawl of bark and bringing 'fairy gifts' to those in need. Neither young nor old believed in that, not even those who still lived on their very own homegrown food and were more than strange.

The young ate imported food. They did not know how to grow a thing, and if they ever did, then they filmed it to illustrate they were an exception to the rule. Many times, when Bothelford thought and dreamed, if it dreamed, it dreamt of farms. It recalled the screams of pigs in its slaughterhouses, it remembered the culling of badgers, the cruel pageantry of fox-hunts in its woods. Bothelford had been most itself in the production of cooked meats, from the calf slain by its master with a blade to the cutting up of its loins for barons and merchants to the feeding of peasant families on its remains to the emptying of plates as second hymns to God were said over the grace of that evening.

The trade routes established by the empire made inadequate the palate of the area; even potatoes—originally an American crop—were not given birth to by the land of Bothelford. Progress took its course. The almost imaginary world of foreign farms and distant goods and many thousands of aeroplanes and ships and production lines became so massive that most who lived off of them in Bothelford generally regarded the food that they consumed as simply blossoming into existence, much in the same way that a young boy imagines babies to emerge of their own accord from the Earth. In these years, all the intimacy which grew from desperation was lost.

Bothelford was a polytechnic converted into a university, an understaffed hospital, a barren, ruined mine, a half-polluted river, and a Dark Age church. But it was first a set of farms. First, it was grain, maize, fertile soil, and potentially an Earth goddess. About seventy years ago, an archaeologist had investigated the area for engravings of a 'Demeter-equivalent goddess' on the side of the mine's entrance. This entrance existed perhaps long before the development of dynamite—the cave or shrine of a divinity that money, hunger, and hope saw fit to destroy during the Victorian era. After it was blown up, the sealed iron and coal within became available. Bothelford doubled in size.

The elder Jeremiah, the only still-living man of English descent with such an irrefutably Old Testament name in the town, came up with the theory at the age of ninety-seven that there had lived a pagan community in the town once. He said it must have confronted the Great Heathen Army (known colloquially as the Vikings) and yet had not, *could not* join them in an alliance against Anglo-Saxon Christianity. Such were their religious differences, these villagers of what became Bothelford, that they would rather establish their own stone castles, their own temple—probably the wrecked ceremonial cave—before lifting their own hammers and sharpening their own axes against the North to face the Viking scourge. Yet if Bothelford dreamed of the cult of its forebears, if it yelled in its stones for the awakening of strange carvings older than Christ and Rome, the town did so rarely at the beginning of the twenty-first century. For there were so few worth speaking to. Or perhaps it dreamed of the old cult constantly, thinking all the time of the forgotten past.

Of 'the castle', which might not have been a castle at all, there remained a grass blob, or artificial hillock, and some large stones with markings that were more likely the scratches produced by the blade of a disobedient shepherd than runes of a priest. By the river, which the town faced sneeringly from its hill, there had been discovered more recently—in the last twenty years—gravestones recording a primordial tongue. So the burial site had come first. The church had come second. Bothelford, like so many other places, was blessed by the religion of Christ while the roots of its oldest trees trembled with the darkness of a different faith. Whether in a site like this, Marine Emery, as a living woman, once lived and spoke was anyone's guess. What is the Frisian or even Old East Norse equivalent of '*I know what it is that happens ...*'?

All this was remembered in the never forgetting ground of Bothelford. And even if every elder died and every youth forgot, someday the folk instinct of that place would come back. Independent bands would invent weird instruments inspired by the wind blowing through the rows of poplars around the castle. Artists would seek to root themselves among the stones before painting images of bees. The grass verges would call to the footsteps of babes. Even drunk teenagers visited the broken alcove at the front of the mine once in a generation. And to them, sometimes, even the mine called, though its furnaces had long lain asleep, 'What would it mean to *really* work hard?'

All this could be so again, though there were but fragments of ruins, if only someone could hear and listen to the world under the town, the seeds from which its now extensive, decaying branches, mutilated with glass and concrete, first grew. But most didn't care.

Did the forgetting begin in the imperial era? This was when Bothelford's best and boldest men were drawn off to distant parts of the British Empire to decimate but also to civilise whole other tribes of people that did not even come into the imagination of the town. Yet the old times passed, and in time, Bothelford was no longer Bothelford. It became a collection of useful men that the new imperium of Britain would find useful for itself. Many days, Bothelford dreamed, if it could dream, of being the feeder fish on the side of a great white shark rather than an entity—an older *Pagan* entity—in its own right. Even great white sharks it had heard of only through the whisperings of Victorian schoolboys with printed textbooks, with diagrams that put the old medieval etchings of sharks, those strange sea beasts, into a kind of professional shame. The old drawings, the old songs, the whispers of the biblical leviathan, and more ancient sea serpents had no register of fact anymore next to these neat informative pictures of jaws and their diameters, these numbers, this diligent inorganic employment of words. Embarrassed perhaps at the stupid old stories that had little to no use anyway and did not deserve to be taught, between the middle of the nineteenth and the twentieth century, the children of Bothelford forgot most of the old tales, even the tales of England and Britain. They did not teach them when they themselves grew up. Marine Emery remained because, believe it or not, she kept coming back, appearing in the church with supernatural regularity.

After much agricultural chaos, much leakage of its population to North America and Canada—India, once in a while, Bothelford was punished for reaping the rewards of empire, for the massive stretch of the British lion's claws into part of every continent on the planet. The mechanisation of farming, the decline of infant mortality, the desolation of medieval feudalism, the availability of better gowns and clothes, and more bread for even poor women—all this depended on the transformation of men into cells in the body of the lion. No more were they men in their own right, citizens and locals of Bothelford, but weapons to be wielded in the name of the imperial crown if only her majesty or the oligarchy behind her so demanded. Hence war eventually. Hence international war, the Great War, and the transformation of so many cells of the lion into dead men. And then another war.

In the newer sections of the graveyard around St Michael's, barely one hundred years old, were the white war graves of at least five hundred men, the others cremated and memorialised by writing on a wall. So similar were these graves, so uniform, that those who first mourned them had the impression that the dead they represented were not even human beings in death. They had become parts of an enormous legion of machines. They had driven machines and fought machines, and they had psychologically become machines inside them, in their brains.

They were meant to wage war and die in war, not to fight chivalrously for their own, for Bothelford. Certainly, they had suffered as men, and those who returned home with wounds not seen since the sacking of the Vikings continued to suffer as men. But they had gone to war as automata and were buried as such. Upon one grave, due to a design flaw, the name and date had already faded from its white surface, so it came to resemble something chrome and shining from a far distant future of seamless industrial floors. To some extent or another, all of the graves had this strange sheen.

Therefore, after so much agony and the exhaustion of so much money in maintaining the empire and in funding the enterprises of former parts of the empire—most of all the emergent, powerful Americans, Bothelford, like all of Britain, forgot what the purpose was of maintaining the empire to begin with. Bit by bit, the lion released its claws from its former possessions now that London, the beast's own heart, was so war-wounded that it struggled to justify its own existence, let alone holdings in Delhi, Kingston, or Islamabad. When Bothelford dreamed in that period, only 'Kingston' sounded familiar to it, and yet if you could enter that dream and ask it about 'Jamaica', it would have no idea what you were talking about.

As this era of conflict ended, whatever cells remained in the British imperial lion, now nothing more than a tattered, barely sentient head, were absorbed into the body of the American eagle. The eagle dined heartily on Europe with the Russian bear, just as it dined heartily on the debts of Bothelford. Soon enough, its wings would swell so obesely over the surface of the cratered Earth that it would begin to show signs of dropping under its own weight. But these are international concerns. And what concerned Bothelford then was itself. For now—in the aftermath of the Second World War—it had been opened to the men of Delhi, Kingston, and Islamabad who, under the British Nationality Act of 1948, could come to Bothelford, though they did not come from Bothelford or know the ways of Bothelford, but those of Delhi, Kingston, and Islamabad. These men, formerly conquered by the most terrifying British, now saw the opportunity to take their place in the dying heart, the heart that was as welcoming as it was soft.

So many had heard hymns of London in their Nigerian, Indian, and Pakistani schools. So much work had the missionaries done to export Anglo-Christianity to the rest of the world that now the rest of the world felt magnetised towards Britain, even after the empire was done with. Perhaps, in many cases, it was *because* the empire was done with that they wanted to come—and after their era of civilisation and submission, they, the colonised, the crucified, wanted revenge on London, and England, and Britain, and Bothelford, according to their *own* ways. Much of their hatred began as unconscious and gradually became conscious. Yet some of it was from the start self-aware, disciplined, and smiling about what was to come.

Whatever residues there were in these former colonial populations who now came to colonise London, and eventually, Bothelford, some were always terrible. The races and the cultures that had produced the Thuggee murder cult, the Haitian

Revolution, sati, and the crazed warrior women who gutted with knives many a British soldier, this deluge who had looked on the pale, blonde wife of the Viceroy and thirsted after her, then they saw fit to obtain the only opportunity they would ever have of possessing her descendants in revenge. And in the dark of the night, the first night one of these rapes was perpetuated against the Master's children, they felt it was revenge.

They had been allowed into England because England truly believed in Christian Liberalism, which posited that all men, all the wretched of the Earth, deserve the same prosperity regardless of their qualities and virtues. But they had brought themselves, their heaving masses, for revenge, amongst other things. Revenge, like the Pagans of Bothelford once wrought, was long forgotten by the English. And so, eventually, in the rubble of Bradford, in the stabbed signs of Peckham, in what would become of Bothelford, it was just revenge, *their* revenge. And more than revenge; there were things that were done to the wives and daughters of England that their husbands and sons would not want to revenge, could not revenge, because they could not imagine them.

As imperial success had furnished such 'revenge', so it brought Bothelford the ingenuity of inventions from the world over and the despair they carried with them.

The first television was stored in the front of a shop. Many came to watch. There were three networks during the Second World War, though all were one in the hubbub of their message (*fight it!*). A bard of the town, Robert Brennam, long since forgotten, had written of the TV press that they 'saw fit to inform in place of telling the truth'. The truth, which you might infer, he supposed came from the stirring up of folklore and in making appeals to archaic wood carvings and hand-drawn maps of the world. For most, his words were as redundant as the idea that the Earth was at the centre of the universe, that the stars told a story, and that, in place of their own increasingly ironic Protestantism, time was not linearly awaiting the arrival of Christ. No, he supposed, time was cyclical! He went to his grave unmourned.

Meanwhile, the TV seemed to have been invented and celebrated everywhere at once. Large vans delivered one, then another, then another, under the cover of night, unseen, unknown. They were brought in like prisoners, like terrorist cells. On what day were they activated? Where was the big switch that the mastermind pressed? They were established over the course of weeks, not months, as an ordinary part of life. Their hypnotism justified their own dominion, rewrote past history in order to include them. Brains were unwound. There was the world before the screens came in, and then there was the world electrified. It was turned on. Screens appeared in the living rooms of houses. Ghost voices chattered through cold nights and warm nights. At first, you might have assumed the population of the town had doubled. There was much more noise. But then, as pubs emptied, as men ceased their ball games beyond puberty, as women did not leave their houses to visit friends, to mind other children, but defaulted from life, paralysed before the light, complaining ever increasingly to their own children about getting 'square eyes', you would have assumed it had halved. That half had died.

How did this happen? The ghosts on the screens first overwhelmed the town, migrating into its offices and bars relentlessly. Then they began to possess the bodies of the living, diminishing their own number in turn. The lights went out of their eyes. Drowsy faces, like the limp bodies of fish, pressed up against pub tables for the match of the day. The phones came later. But by then, men were already more excited on such occasions than by their own wives. Some dreamed that each TV had limbs and arms of its own, could love, could hate, could instruct such love and hatred from its viewers that it might as well do so! Well then, was TV more capable of hate or love? In its ecstatic glow, few ever wondered.

Those that felt the majority of people were ugly, that it would not be worth looking the checkout lady in the eye, who did not want to engage in the tiresomeness of human relationships, who were born oglers, who could love—in a deep enough sadness—the image of a woman before a real one, those that sought pleasure, those who had never received the encouragement necessary to make them want to try, to make them want to be fathers or mothers, having none worthy of their own, even in the fifties, they willed this global gift into existence. And it replaced most things. The colonial genius of the English and of the Americans, their children, turned on itself. The mind was laid bare. Its several regions, its imaginary lands, its strange territories, its sexual paraphilias, all were stimulated. Most were mined for great electric joys.

The outgrowth of feminism, of women seeing that labour no longer relied on any real separation of the sexes, or at least believing that to be so, entwined in this device. The shameful, embarrassing, undesirable male majority became subject to recordings, to rumours, to more gossip than their forefathers had ever known. This fear, inseminated in the youth of the twenty-first century since the inception of puberty, led the image of the female to triumph in the mind of the male over the real thing. The male phantom of money and the female phantom of ideology made love with each other during this period like scarcely any young men or women of Bothelford.

There was also a third power involved: denial. For it was always easier for the sorry, pale victims of these spirits to turn to their phones, to consuming and making porn, than ever to acknowledge their displacement and the ongoing colonisation of Bothelford by the families of Delhi, Kingston, and Islamabad. Few even allowed themselves to imagine that the black mother with three babies who passed by their window, followed by an older white mother with only one, might mean something overwhelmingly significant. As for the war memorial in the centre of Bothelford, a tall limestone design with a Celtic cross shooting up from it, none disturbed the Arab who sat there and smoked and poured Red Bull on the names of the men, the dates of their deaths. None even thought of him. Minds glimpsed him and deleted him, having learned how to neglect the real world for the phone.

During the fifties and sixties, when many of the first interracial rapes entered Britain shortly after the docking of Windrush and Notting Hill burst with fury as a number of black men were found pimping out pale-faced, drugged women, the papers, then the television, then the schools worked tirelessly to install the contrary attitude. They put the issue on ice, forever. They installed a mechanism of surrender in Britain, in England, in Bothelford—in the children of each, so that, despite everything that occurred around them, and everything that the foreign, colonising populations would do, especially to women, the natives would lie inert. Sometimes they would actually say sorry.

Here, the lessons that the descendants of the British imperialists had learned from controlling and subduing distant nations were used to subjugate those that did not have the money to keep moving to vanishingly whiter towns. Whether or not a foreign power, or an ancient hatred of the English, was involved in this process was unknown to most. And yet the English Christian Liberals (now more Liberal than Christian) were *consumed* by the foreign logic of colonial revenge. In truth, they were so eaten up by it that they would lead invading armies against their own, and plan and volunteer to serve in 'refugee' schemes whilst smiling over the dilapidation of towns filled with vile Brexiteers more closely related to them than any other group of people on Earth. Certainly, the hatred of middle-class upstarts for the humble origins of their forebears served the effacement of England wonderfully when many of them began to funnel into government during the seventies and eighties.

And did they have a plan, a plan to do all of this? If not a plan, there was a tendency, a demonic impulse, that might as well have been one. For it was decided, without being stated, that the political class would trade one group of subject working people for another and in enriching themselves by lowering the cost of labour, feel that they were saving the world from the dreaded white race. Therefore, 'revenge' continued uninterrupted for three generations, and nobody in power, lest they call forth the ghost of Adolf Hitler or the unsightly implication of being working class (and so unavoidably aware of race), ever said a word. How many thousands of white children were raped, beaten, and in some cases mutilated beyond recognition, or impregnated by cackling foreign men, was never investigated. For peace and the dreams of Liberals, it stayed unknown.

Yet Bothelford had nightmares. When, for example, Bothelford dreamed of Natalie McPherson, bound to a table by four cousins from Hyderabad, and used as a device for their enjoyment, to the extent that her eyes were bruised, blackened, and she was so unable to process what had happened to her that her parents discovered her hanging body when she was only thirteen, then it dreamed madly and it screamed in its sleep and it tried to scratch out one of its own eyes, or a young man who lived in it did. Slowly, painfully, Bothelford was going insane. Bothelford was itself being shredded and torn up and uprooted, and though nobody spoke of it, let alone anyone in London—a place already mad, the truth was felt, deeply, agonisingly, like a stomach ulcer inside every Englishman, an open wound in the hearts of fathers and sons. Young white men looked at each other in pubs, once in a while, and knew what had happened somewhere in Bothelford. They also knew, or felt, that they were occupied, as the colonies of Britain had once been occupied, to which the only appropriate response would be revolt. For if the logic of revenge held that Pakistan could ravage England's daughters for their being conquered, then there would come a time when the colonial rebellion of the English would be justified, for they, for 'we', would be a subject population. And on the first appearance of the spectre of Marine Emery in St Michael's in that decade, in the year 2005, the man of a hundred years who confronted her with his grandson saw the red halo that famously hovered behind her, dripping with blood.

The seeds of future ethnic violence had been sewn, though few could describe their gestation, who and where they had come from, why they were beginning to sprout and grow, flower redly like knife wounds in the sides of flannel shirts. Yet despite being aware of Bothelford's deterioration more than most, or perhaps because she could already picture to herself the new dawn that ridiculously waited on the other side of it all, the waitress Mary Phillips, descended from the local singer Theresa, decided that she would have a child instead of going to university. Her parents protested that this was not what they wished, not good for her future due to her potential, and yet she knew what she wanted. She married a man named John Grundon. The couple would divorce after she found him in bed with another woman one drunken night. But when she felt her child kick within her, Mary could not say she regretted her decision.

In Bothelford, late in the year 2007, Jack Grundon was born. He had a long nose, brown hair, and blue eyes. He stared in wonder at everything before him like many a child. His first memory, recalled by him even as an old man, formed two years later when he stood in the shower, stared through the Tudor windows in his mother's house into her bright green garden, and saw the sun play along the sprayed water near to his eyes.

It might have been a glorious childhood and a wonderful life, but little did he know what had already happened and, because of that, what was going to happen to him.

TWO

For Jack Grundon, education began much earlier than school. This is true of everyone, but an important part of Jack's education came from smallholding, the hobby his mother, Mary, developed of looking after chickens. She would not permit him to get a dog, despite his constant 'badgering', as she called it. His first glance at his father's old sci-fi comics, featuring a brave, always-masked sentinel and his cybernetic hound, made him want one—a great companion that he could sail on adventures with over the whole world. But his mother did not like dogs. She had been bitten by a dalmatian near a park bench by her old school in Bothelford, a fact which led her to initially get on well with her neighbour Fatima, who also hated dogs, who had even said once that they were cursed. Well, Mary *said* they got on. Fatima was quiet, and she wore a burqa. Her husband was almost always with her, although Mary did not know his name, and he did not bother to introduce himself. Neither man nor wife commented, however, when she decided to buy her chickens. She had had English neighbours in the past who would have complained ceaselessly about the presence of such apparently dirty animals. In those days, she supposed the silence was welcome from the other house. Years before, the two houses had been one. Then one of the owners in the nineteen-sixties had gotten the idea of breaking the house up into two so that he could earn more in rent. As a result, the walls were sometimes quite thin between Fatima's house and Mary and Jack's; they had been crudely added on with none of the talent of the house's original builder. Yet even when, late at night, the TV blazed above the empty fireplace of their own living room, no sound ever seemed to enter from Fatima's on the other side. Sometimes Mary wondered what this meant. But not too often.

As for smallholding, Jack was introduced to the chickens Betty and Betsy when he was four and a half years old. It was 2012. His mother would check for eggs in the henhouse she had purchased for the birds in the back garden and wash up their trays of poo, and sometimes Jack would help. Jack would pet the chickens and kiss them also, even if they didn't really want to be. He would enjoy playing with them when they jumped on his shoulders as he changed their grain and water with his mother. They were not dogs, but he loved them as his own. He was the age where love like that is possible. They kept them for four years.

Yet though Fatima's house remained as quiet as ever, his own living room changed in 2016. There were many evenings when the TV seemed to blaze all night. His mother would occasion-ally shout at the screen, as if instructed by it, and he would cry from her shouting, and then she would apologise, call a friend angrily on the phone, and then apologise once more.

And that is how things were for a while. He would wake in the morning. He would hold the Orpington feathers of Betty and Betsy, his mother would drop him at the nursery (a few years later he would go to the local primary school where he'd be given colouring pens by strange young women who were like his mother and yet were not his mother), and then he would return, be presented with a microwaved lasagne usually, before his mother would hold him and shriek at the TV, at an American political leader halfway around the world. It was a strange time. And once returning with his mother from a trip to a nearby farm, where he had seen pigs for the first time, he had glimpsed Fatima in a full-length niqab. He had blinked. He had looked again. And there she was.

Jack learned from this cycle of days to fear the screen, to feel dependent, as he was, on his mother, and that in the left side of the house, in what he called 'the Other side of the house', there lived strangers. There were people with dark skin who rarely spoke, some of whom wore what Jack perceived as masks—as some characters and puppets wore on *CBeebies*—and who did not really want to speak to you ever. Jack also learned and remembered for the rest of his life that TV essentially controlled the adults he met. During visiting weekends, when he was presented to his father, though always gripped tightly by his mother, his father would stare with the same mesmerised look at the screen in his own flat—a tight, unkempt interior. It was as if by staring at it, his eyes were seeing through into another world.

Even as a boy, Jack Grundon judged his parents, then appearing like all-providing gods before him, to be but lesser gods before the screen. And that was the true god, although the family was split, because both sides watched it! Once Jack had pressed his hands on the low screen of his father, trying to enter it, trying to get inside that bright place in which so many glorious things seemed to reside. And when he had heard the story of the archaeologist Howard Carter, how he had opened the tomb of Tutankhamun and seen such beautiful ancient things he could not describe, Jack saw in his mind the world of the TV again. Having heard it from his father, this story quickly became Jack's favourite. But every time he heard it, even if he did not remember it, it was not the world of pharaohs, of Anubis, of Bastet, or an afterlife of reeds that stirred in his mind, but again the simple, flat, flashing screen. He had been kept from iPads by his parents in case they interfered with his ability to read, his curiosity in books, or his appreciation for the smell of the spring air and the sounds of birds. By that time, they had heard stories of technologically addicted teenagers who could do little more than consume pornography, let alone read. And so they had catastrophised, kept him from acquiring a phone or touch pad. And yet the TV, even in a period where its influence was being steadily diluted by the smartphone, had Jack ensnared. He knew that whatever was on it must be true—or true enough to change the minds of his parents like the lights in his room were switched off by either one of them at night.

What of Jack's time in the local primary school? Little can match the significance of TV. But school was the first time he met other children, there being none to play with in his area but those of Fatima, who did not want to play. Jack was an emotional boy, and when in his favourite lesson with Miss Wright, who was teaching the class that term about Egyptian mythology, he forgot the name of his favourite god— the jackal-headed one!—then he had cried and cried. He loved the dark ideas of a different land, of powers distinct from the boring Anglican church, St Michael's, where he had been made to go with his grandparents *so* often. He even wondered some nights what it would be like if he were born again with the powers of Anubis over life and death. He decided if he were reborn with those powers, crossing his fingers, he would have to be good.

But these lessons, which he adored, though he wept in them, couldn't last either. Some parents had complained that an education in a theology that challenged the beliefs of the ten per cent Muslim minority in the class was misleading, unnecessary, and, at worst, harmful. Miss Wright listened and obeyed their instructions without protest. When addressing these concerns at Parents' Evening, she decided to sweep back her hair in a bun and dye what had been her streaks of bright pink an unassuming black. They would pursue the course she had wanted to follow from the beginning rather than what Mrs Nott had postulated, had forced her to teach: this education in Ancient Egyptian lives that stank of British imperial attitudes of fascination with a colonised other, of the minds and souls of violent young boys.

Jack didn't see it, but once—and she thought of it even then at Parents' Evening, gleefully—Miss Wright had held his friend

Thomas aside, had taken him out of class for a minute when he came in one morning. She had stripped the England shirt that he had worn to class and found him a pale blue one from lost property to put on instead. Whatever complaint Thomas's parents made as a result of this went unheeded, and in all likelihood, it wasn't even made. Because they too were watchers of television, and they too were aware of the direction in which the culture had been moved and what could be said, what could not; who mattered, and who did not, though this they couldn't say, deprived as they were of even the words to say it—transmitted, as all important *true* words had to be, through the TV and, failing that, the news media on the smartphone.

In 2016, words were scarcely as important as the films, documentaries, and newsreels that served as their prerequisites, as the framing devices for making the words make sense, make any sense at all. Jack, a child, did not know any of this, and yet he felt it. It affected his life like the lessons of Jesuit priests had the life of his great-uncle in the seminary, and perhaps more deeply. The blitz of 'education' to which he was submitted was constant between the ages of five and nine. Miss Wright had her liberalising way, as did others, although Mrs Nott did not. She was the 'tight arse', as Miss Wright privately called her, who wanted to read such punitive classics as *The Water-Babies*, a story that featured a Mrs Bedonebyasyoudid, who covered children in spikes when they disobeyed. Nothing like that could be tolerated.

No, Miss Wright and her faction—adequately funded and represented on the local school board—*demanded* that the opposite tendency be embraced. She had failed a master's in education at Glasgow University, and yet her experimentalism, her desire to dissolve gender, to mark the children which she had not had with *her* lessons was so potent, like in the case of so many others, even then, that she would not, could not compromise. She knew what she wanted to do. For all but her cherished Muslim students, who were immune to the logic of revenge, which was reserved for those she regarded, like herself, as would-be white oppressors, Pride month was insisted on. Lessons on Queerness were taught to crowds of white six-year-olds. Sex education was smuggled in seven years early. Diagrams of penises alienated from the male body were brandished in front of Holly and Natalie, as were vaginas and cartoon diagrams of lubricated anuses before Tom and Jack and Oliver. More often than not, the sex acts that were portrayed and the films that were shown, provided proudly by any number of charities, featured black men with white women and white men with other white men, brown men, or no one. The white men would also sometimes be dressed up as women, and cartoon women with scar marks where their breasts had been surgically removed were shown to the same extent to the little girls. Miss Wright had gotten in on the best of it all early! Sometimes she caught herself crossing herself for the contacts she had made in her old department, the books that she had read, before countering that gesture with some curse from Hecate or whomever that she dearly wanted to come more naturally. Oh well.

The end goal of this 'education' was neither stated aloud nor did Miss Wright ever think of it in secret within her own mind. She just knew that what was happening in the United States, as the TV had told her, was very *deeply* wrong, and that the 'racism' of the American President had to be counteracted with radical queer liberation. Further than that, the charities that published her blogs and paid for her campaigns in the local area (whether the money came from Manchester or New York) believed in her and that all this was necessary and heroic. Even though there was no heaven apart from perhaps the paradise of her Muslim darlings, who had been and were being victimised by whites, this was her chance to illustrate that she was Good: *to steal the young from the repressive habitats of their parents, to remake them in her own proudly unreproductive image.*

This had a number of consequences. When the Muslim boys were in her class, usually a little older than Jack or Thomas, they used the words 'racist', 'privileged', 'white', and even 'bitch' constantly, and were as far as any white person could tell at that age—before the requisite guilt had been transmitted into them by the TV or the newspaper or the classroom—fully encouraged in this by Miss Wright or Miss Thorne or Mx. Lynn, who always rolled pink jumper sleeves over her serpent tattoos on Parents' Night and would frequently sit in during Miss Wright's lessons. Before 2020, at least for this little set of empowered intellectuals, all was moving splendidly along in the right direction. Their 'programming' had already started moulding their young clients in different ways than anyone would have expected. All was well.

Then a Chinese virus triggered a year and a half of quarantine all over the world, and Jack Grundon was forced to sit before the knees of his parents drinking and watching yet more TV, using phones yet more, and listen to his mother banging pans out in the night at 9 p.m. to celebrate the work being done by the National Health Service like an Aztec priestess before a sacrificed head. That would accelerate his development, if it could be called that. But it was not yet time, as it became in some schools in 2025, for teaching students about furries, about animal identities, about embracing the fandoms some Generation Z teachers had joined and found the relief of fetishism in during their own teens. All that was well on its way by the time Jack, at eight, had simply decided to stare out of the bright summer windows of his primary school instead of paying any mind to the words that were spoken, shaken out of the mouths of strange females that had neither a place in the real world nor accomplished anything of value in his dreams.

He took to making sounds in his class. He took to drawing shapes that offended. He had been told not to speak of the church, not to draw a crucifix, because it was exclusionary, offensive. He had seen a hammer and sickle on the side of Mx. Lynn's laptop and liked it enough to sketch it. She had smiled at him. And he had drawn a cross next to it. Though he had been told constantly never to draw guns, nor compete with Rafiq or Aman in the drawing of guns, he drew thousands of guns. He drew pistols and spears. He read detailed maps on the front table of his mother's semi-detached house. He wondered why the globe, the old autumnal globe in the spare room of the main building, was never used. He wanted to feel and turn its little squeaky wheel. He strove to feel out the continents he had only been presented with in passing. He felt, when his mother brought him her own globe from his grandmother's, that he was looking over the whole round Earth from the perspective of a great, weird giant. There was what was taught, and then there was what was known. There was playing with twigs in the snow even with Rafiq and his older brother—who called Jack kafir, whatever that meant—and then there were documentaries, lectures, sermons of doubt. There was action, and then there were words. Most words were lies.

The first day he was sent home from school, the first of many, he had run out of the class when Miss Wright told him to sit and listen to a discussion about white privilege that, of course, Rafiq and Aman found absolutely hilarious. It was as if the windows had called him outside, that the sun had throbbed all day, for so many days, for so many youthful eternities already that could never come back to him, and he wanted to see his chickens again. Tacitly, with as much strategy as he possessed, he left the room, he made a scene outside, he wept and cried. His mother had to come and drive over and scold him after hearing Miss Wright's account, and then she and Jack had gone back home. But when Jack arrived, he embraced his dear birds, providers of his eggs, providers of the pancakes his mother cooked, and fell asleep and waited for tomorrow, when more or less the same thing, but without protest, without kicking up a fuss, was going to happen again. Because nothing ever changed. Because he felt even then that there was no escape from his life, from the 'usefulness' of school, from the rooms of his parents, and from the money which he did not understand, but everything, literally everything, was organised to accrue.

'Why do I have to go to school?' he had once asked, more curious than nagging.

His mother replied, 'Because if you don't, you'll never get a job.'

Yet there was so much in school that couldn't have anything to do with earning money, could it? The distance that he remained from the whole adult world and all its secrets, he supposed, must provide some justification for his ignorance. Surely, when he grew up, it would all make sense. Because, Jack felt, if education couldn't justify itself economically, or for the sake of making him productive or wealthy, what *actually* was education? What was it but a carefully devised set of extremely boring, time-sapping rituals designed to keep him from the world, his birds, the sun? When he saw photographs of early-twentieth-century Boy Scouts, now defunct in Bothelford, he wondered if the impulse he had felt draw him to the old autumnal globe might have been developed—educated, as it were—in another era.

He came to realise it would have been so, and that that solar impulse might have been the centre of his education, rather than the most distantly opposed feeling, only midway through secondary school. Sealed in the sterile laboratory of classrooms for a sufficient number of years, he was sometimes amazed to remember the taste of the air. By that time, his hands had no connection to the land. Every magical ancestral thread that had tried to guide his digits to the soil, to *his* earth, or to the dreams of ships, cutlasses, and kingdoms had been cut away, cleft by the invisible blade of an educator. By sixteen, keyboards had taught him the contrary instinct. They had deformed his hands into clasping, rheumatic claws that hurt in the night.

But it was when Jack was twelve, even before the pandemic, that the earliest true lesson of his life was taught. This was the lesson of Betty and Betsy, his ridiculous teachers, when he awoke one day to screams from the chicken coop. He was brushing up and down a small grass verge in Mary's back garden. His mother was on the phone inside, laughing with a friend about something she had seen on TV, and he had stumbled to the wire-mesh cage at the other side of the garden as one mesmerised. The jet of orange, white, and red that shot from the enclosure and past him was unlike anything he had seen before, yet as he touched the blood scattered on the ground, let his sight linger on the strewn gizzards, and approach, stumbling nearer, what remained of the dear birds he had received in the place of a dog, he knew it had been a fox. He did not even yell, for he could not believe what he was looking at. He pressed his little face up against the wire. He let it cling there, redden as the bars chafed the top of his scalp. There were the heads of Betty and Betsy. One of the beaks was snapped to a cartoonish extent. He wanted to touch it and check if it was real but did not want to allow himself to feel her yellow, busted jaw, her devoured comb. It was as if they had been beheaded. An entity—not a predator, but an entity—had entered the henhouse and beheaded his chickens, both of them. It was not one at a time but both, in one go. The lesson of Betty and Betsy, the lesson that most chickens retain within them for anyone unlucky enough to lose one after elevating them to the status of a pet, was that life was cheap, that everything could end nastily, quickly, that there was no magic armour that prevented you and your pets, or, for that matter, your people, from being cut up and extinguished like so many others in history. Death was real.

Things were not as they were in the cartoons, where no one ever died nowadays, or in the children's books that he had been read. In his mind, Jack felt an immense stage curtain peel back before the splattered henhouse. He recalled, even then, the shedding of great curtains from the local pantomime that he had gone to see every Christmas of his life with, for once, both his mother and father. Now, however, what was revealed was not a wedding scene from *Beauty and the Beast* or *Aladdin* but the black hole that had always been behind all living things. He realised in that moment that animals compete for life, that the state of nature is inseparable from a state of horror, that evil exists in the appetite of one thing for another, and that no animal—even his, even Betty and Betsy—is invulnerable to becoming someone's food. As these thoughts he could not put into words rose within him, so did his yelling until his mother put down her phone, came outside, and saw what had happened. She held him so tightly she almost cried herself. And yet she was cold. And yet she had always known that something like this could happen, had happened on her own grandmother's farm.

Maybe it was due to the fact that children in 2019 were not supposed to be exposed to the cycle of life and death as their ancestors had, or she supposed this to be the case, which caused her to read him Christian material for the next few days. Although he had never received an Anglican baptism, let alone an instruction in the story of Christ bar the whisperings of his grandmother, now, on the verge of the pandemic, he began to hear stories of the Magi following the star, of the Massacre of the Innocents, of Christ's healing powers, of his meeting the Devil in the desert, of the stations of the cross, and of Christ's return, and from William Blake, how these events might have taken place in England, all to soften the truth of what had happened to his two birds. The fact that he learnt Blake's *Jerusalem*—about the presence of Christ in England—was, again, due to his grandmother's influence. For his mother, the story of the poem sounded all too like an English version of Mormonism, but whatever soothed the sensitivity of her boy, whatever numbed him to the pulling apart of life was good enough. That Christmas, she decided to buy him the iPad that for so long he had asked her to get for him. He was no longer prohibited.

Little did she know that a quietness had crept into her son that would not be removed for the rest of his life nor that the coming two years of playing with his iPad, of not reading, of receiving little to no meaningful education through Zoom calls, during Lockdown, would deepen it substantially. She knew, to her credit, that he wanted to be an 'adventurer', whatever that meant. Wherever that idea had come from, she knew John, his father, had something *probably* to do with it—if it wasn't just the dream of every male to go forth and explore distant lands.

Once she and Jack had watched *The Truman Show* together as she poured herself a heavy glass of wine. This was two months into the pandemic, in which Jack lost his grandfather Francis on his father's side, a Catholic, but for whom no funeral had been allowed. She glared at her boy and wondered whether the death of this man could ever affect him like the death of his birds. On the TV, a scene played in which Truman sat in class as a young lad and asked about exploring the far-off parts of the world, said that he wanted to go to Fiji, and she had instinctively, proudly tapped Jack on the shoulder. She didn't remember the purpose of the scene in the film: in all likelihood, it was to set up the main character's imprisonment in modern life. But what happened next was that the stern teacher character told the young Truman that the whole world had been explored already, that there was nowhere for him to adventure left, and then Mary Phillips had turned off the screen. She drank; she read Jack a poem by Edward Lear before tucking him into bed.

By the time Jack was fourteen years old, Lockdown was over, his mother had complained vociferously about Miss Wright's showing pictures of lynched black bodies on a Zoom call, and Fatima had had two more children, although no one noticed, he was largely unable to read physical books anymore. Either he had to have headphones playing surging, ambient music, or he had to have the glow of the iPad to process anything. The books on his mother's shelves, purchased almost exclusively for his amusement from local charity shops and going from Ladybird books for early readers up through *The Hobbit* and

The Lord of the Rings—all these were like so much waste paper to him now without some form of additional stimulation. He couldn't imagine anyone reading them unmediated, and few around him, whether his mother, his father, or the children in his class, ever actually did. Whatever the past was, it was alien, so different from now that he could neither identify with those who were part of it nor find any particular reason why learning about it was immediately significant. There was then, and there was now, and there was, in the future, the return of Jesus Christ to save him from the death that had come to his birds—which he knew, for they had died and for he had thought them immortal, could be meted out to almost anyone. Jack began to think of darkness constantly.

Once, on an Autumn night, he dreamed he was in the centre of Bothelford before the big war memorial, that the sun was a gigantic red orb, and that the streets were filled with statues, petrified human beings whom he knew, aunts and uncles. Seated at the top of the memorial was a monster, a *chimera*, with a television for a head and a dripping, red mouth of teeth. In the dream, Jack tried to remember which video games he had played the night before to inspire these images, but nothing exactly fitted. He was somehow aware he was in a dream and yet couldn't influence its contents whatsoever. The chimera with the flashing rectangular face and the red jaws spoke to him some distorted lines his mother had read him from the poet Percy Bysshe Shelley. It declared itself to be Bothelford's 'King of Kings', sovereign over this zone for its amusement.

What was playing on its screen-head played too fast for him to recognise more than snatches of a girl in a red jacket, a dark-faced man with moon-white teeth, the raising of hammers and cricket bats outside the school—or, yes, his mother's school. It was a strange dream, and when he woke up from it and on a walk passed the war memorial again only to see the delusional drunk Arab who sat there usually, Jack felt both satisfied that the monster he dreamed of wasn't real as well as concerned, in his imaginative way, that this man, whoever he was, was but another form of the chimera. Why a chimera? *Something mixed, something that didn't belong, yet was all.*

Jack was walking through the town centre to collect some groceries with his mother when he stopped and stared at the Arab. His mother had tugged him along, and yet he stayed in place. Who was this man who sat where the school visited on Remembrance Day? What, if he was not some chimera, some weird monster who abided by rules differently than everyone else, gave him the excuse to sit there, to smoke, to ... soil himself there? Because when he stood up and looked down over Jack and his mother as the chimera had looked down on Jack in his own dream, Jack could see a black-brown stain on the smooth stone behind him, next to a roll of toilet paper.

The Arab turned and stared at Mary's breasts. 'White *pus*-sy!' he said, as if spitting.

'What?' said Jack.

His mother dragged him off to the town centre and didn't look back, and the Arab sat and drank and smoked another cigarette from his several opened packets.

At the supermarket, they bought some bottles of water, two loaves of bread, some carrots, some semi-skimmed milk, and some cornflakes, and his mother snatched from the side two bottles of whiskey and one bottle of wine. Later on she bought, though she had to get the Indian cashier to help her get them from behind a plastic case, a pair of scissors that as soon as they left she immediately put into her pocket. Jack remembered her asking for 'mace', but as soon as the cashier expressed that he did not understand what that was, she dropped the issue. They left, walking approximately a mile and a half around the war memorial on which the name of Sergeant Maurice Grundon had been inscribed, commemorating his service at Passchendaele. Whether it was his name that had been defecated on or someone else's scarcely mattered to Mary Phillips. She just wanted to get home safe.

One week later, a year and a half later than he was supposed to due to the pandemic, Jack would start secondary school at the local comprehensive. There had been online sessions here and there from a number of different institutions, but nothing consistent during Lockdown. Jack was going to have to join late. He would have only a short time to prepare for GCSEs, on top of whatever 'education' he had received from crash-course study programmes. In the meantime, as Jack waited for school to begin, he would think much of the past week, of the chimera and the Arab, and also of the fact that he had heard from his mother that some of Fatima's boys would be attending the same school. Had she asked Fatima directly? Well, *no*, she had heard from Patricia at the corner shop that two of Fatima's sons were going to be a year above Jack. Jack was fourteen now, and they would be fifteen or sixteen. Although the school was co-educational, Mary hadn't heard anything about Fatima's daughters, however many she had. Mary guessed three or four. And who was she, in comparison, with her one boy? Sometimes she laughed about it—her golden boy! A great pity it was that he had missed years seven and eight. A pity that Lockdown had eaten away those years, that integration would be so much harder for him now. But that was life.

As for the school, the building was large and had been constructed a decade after the Second World War. It was ugly to look at, excluding the small chapel to which it was attached. The chapel was built out of bright red bricks and was a lesser-known accomplishment of the architect William Butterfield. The school uniform was an appealing blue blazer that Mary said went well with the colour of Jack's eyes, although it clashed, she felt, with both the red brick of the chapel and the smoky grey of the modern, main building. All in all, the place was a chapel attached to a set of oblong storm clouds. Mary could hardly think of it as a school.

Dropping Jack at the gates for the first time, she found herself unable not to feel that she was lowering him into a den of vipers. It wasn't simply the feeling of her child's leaving her—or perhaps merely it was! But perhaps it was not. Perhaps it wasn't what she felt but what she saw. Because at the gate, Fatima's sons (if they were Fatima's sons?) arrived in their own way, with masks, on heavy bikes. They cycled in among twelve or fifteen other Muslim schoolchildren, although they all looked far beyond their ages. When she waved to them and wished them good luck at school, there were a few exchanges in Urdu under their breaths but no greetings returned. Roughly twenty per cent of the children she had seen, she realised, were Arab or black, and roughly a third of those Arab or black children came into school wearing masks and did not seem to speak a word of English.

But Mary remembered Hitler, she remembered Enoch Powell, the secular sin of white racism, and tried not to think about it. She waved Jack off among Bothelford's young, diversifying crowd. Riding home in the car, she had to stop and breathe and open the window. The way that Jack had looked at her with his blue eyes, he—but she couldn't think this!—seemed as if he were imploring her in desperation.

If he could have asked her a question then, have put it to her eloquently, have said to her painfully what he was concerned about, she imagined he would have asked her, 'Why am I being condemned, perhaps for years, to live alongside terrifying young men who clearly have nothing in common with me, who will want nothing more than to prey on my innocence, to make war on me in the playground, to use me like a toy, when you as a child dealt with nothing of the sort?'

But this she could not ever think about.

THREE

Jack Grundon first met Basil Alawi on the third day of school that week. Briefly, they were friends. If the geography of the school was pale and laboratorial, then Basil was dusty and quasi-Victorian. He always wore a pair of expensive-looking glasses or shades when his allergies were triggered and the protection didn't suffice to defend him against all the pollen in England. He could tie three different kinds of ties, his favourite being the Windsor, he said. He immaculately folded a red handkerchief each morning and placed it within his breast pocket. If the colour didn't match the blue uniform, then it certainly complemented the brown tweed jacket that he would always wear over it, even at that apparently young age. He did not seem dangerous.

When Jack was introduced to his form room, spanning every year group in the school, he was sat next to Basil and immediately wondered, although he did not ask directly, about this intelligent-looking boy's ethnic background. He was completely different from the 'balaclava-wearing rabble', Basil's term for the black Muslim students they had both seen kicking each other outside Mr Miles's Physics laboratory. He

was about a head and a half shorter than Jack, as well as half a
head shorter than the other students on average. But whereas
Jack slouched to speak down to others slightly from his height,
Basil's compact dignity meant that those who spoke to him
strangely felt encouraged to stand properly rather than croon
at all. Yes, if Jack could summarise his thoughts on Basil, he
would say that Basil looked like the kind of foreigner who
would have been welcomed into the homes not only of his
own grandparents but also those of the aristocracy of an earlier
period. Or at least that was the impression that Basil worked
tirelessly to leave; so badly did he want to be English.

'You dress very nice,' said Jack across the sleek, sterile table
they shared before the whiteboard.

'Thank you,' said Basil. 'My mother bought me the jacket
from Harrods in London. It's a wonderful place.'

'I've never been,' said Jack. 'What do your parents do?'

'My father's a businessman,' Basil said, quickly sensing what
the real question was behind all Jack's posturing. 'He had to
flee from Syria, from Assad.'

'You mean during the Syrian refugee crisis?'

Basil grinned slightly and shook his head a little.

'No, a while before that. We're Alawites.'

'You're what?'

'—bid'ah!!' Muhammad Akbar, the youngest in their year,
squealed three seats behind them. 'Bid'ah!!' But they paid him
no mind.

'It's a minority religious sect,' Basil said. 'I'm a strange kind
of Muslim. Anyway, when the bossman took over Syria—that's

Assad, the man you see on the news, he had a number of disagreements with my father. That's why I'm here.'

'And is your mother ...'

'Not English,' Basil snickered (oddly, Jack thought, complimented by this). 'She's Syrian also. But what do the Indians call
it ... High Caste. In terms of whiteness, I pale in comparison
next to you.'

'... Bid'ah ...' Muhammad Akbar whispered.

'What does that even mean?' said Jack, thinking about
throttling Muhammad.

'It means he thinks I'm a kind of heretic, as he does you.'

'But I'm not religious,' said Jack.

'Yes, you are,' said Basil and did not explain what he meant.

Later, as the form tutor, Mr Tedbury, decided to read the
daily news and ask for commentary from the students on
matters of potential Lockdowns in future and what the consequences might be if his preferred candidate did not win the
American presidential election— British politics being entirely
shoved to the side, Jack decided he wanted to hear more about
Syria. He wanted perhaps faster than ever before to become
friends with this lad. Basil was quite simply the most interesting person Jack had ever met.

Further than that, Basil's interactions with other Muslims,
especially those wearing the balaclavas whenever they could
(who could only be instructed to remove them in the cafeteria when Mr Hussein walked by), were interesting. At lunch
break, when pressed by Jack on these subjects, although he
felt he might risk offending Basil, Basil responded that he felt

part of their community, part of their struggle. They were not Syrians, and yet he was a fellow non-white, or 'brown person'. He included in this brethren even the Africans that he noted his Tunisian ancestors had enslaved. It was an odd alliance, he acknowledged. Yet they were all 'strangers in England and among the English', whatever that meant. (Jack already thought he knew exactly what this meant.)

When asked, Basil said his dream was to own a Rolls-Royce, to marry an Englishwoman, and, in essence, to achieve what his father's enemy Bashar Al-Assad had achieved with his half-English wife, his dictatorship, his luxury lifestyle, all the while maintaining a quiet, conflict-averse manner like Basil's, apparently. It became obvious over the course of that first day that, whilst Basil did not like talking about Syria, he appreciated Jack's intrigue enough to supplement him with whatever details he wanted. The lessons were boring and empty by comparison.

'And did you know ...' said Basil over a chocolate muffin that his 'friend' Leonard, working behind the café bar, allowed him for free: (Basil had such an irrefutable charm about him that he could seemingly get anyone and at any age to give him little gifts, here and there.) '*Bassel* Al-Assad was initially meant to be ruler of Syria.'

'Really? Are you named after him?' said Jack, eating the croissant that Basil had gotten him for free also.

'I have no idea. And he apparently loved sports cars. He might even have died in a *Fer-rari* accident. I'll have to check his Wikipedia.'

That was the only time that day that Jack got a hint of Basil's foreign accent, which was otherwise so sublimated into Received Pronunciation that he could easily have passed for an upper-class white Englishman over the phone, or at least as one of a higher class than Jack.

At the end of the day, when Jack returned home, sitting in his mother's car, and only giving her the necessary details about how swimming class was great and how the English department in the school actually had a number of lovely books with whales on the covers by a man called Melville he wanted to check out, and that he hadn't been intimidated by the 'bad kids', whoever they were, honest, he closed his mouth and asked himself one thing.

Why, *why* was someone as rich and talented and clever and 'international', for the lack of a better word, as Basil, stuck in his *shitty* comprehensive school?

Why? What had happened? Was he thrown out of a posh school beforehand, or what? It just didn't make sense. He was one of the cleverest people that Jack had ever met, yet, clearly, also older than him. That Jack had figured out, because there was simply no way that Basil was fourteen or fifteen. He had to be sixteen, minimum, to speak as assuredly as he did. Yes, the form groups were mixed, going from nine to sixteen years old, whereas the sixth form went to their own separate form rooms between the ages of seventeen and nineteen. Yet Basil— he found out from the email of a timetable sent to him that Friday—was going to attend *his* English Literature classes with Mr Hussein the next week. What for? Why place someone clearly so wise with people *so* dumb and young? It just didn't make sense, any of it.

Yet when Jack entered the English class on the next Monday, exhausted and burnt out from a whole weekend of browsing his iPad both to distract from the presence of his father and to erase whatever stress he had built up from the previous school week, it became obvious to him that a kind of deal had been struck between Basil and Mr Hussein, or Basil's parents and Mr Hussein, possibly. Over what, Jack Grundon did not know. But Basil and Mr Hussein nodded at each other in a tacit agreement that nobody else, whether white, Arab, or black, seemed to understand. Basil would crouch at the back of his desk and write, it seemed, whatever he wanted to. Jack wondered if he was autistic, needed the additional space to do whatever his genius wished rather than straining himself against classroom norms—although this dynamic was *so* particular it didn't make sense on its own without something secret being involved. But then what was involved?

When the class actually started, Mr Hussein said he wanted to take the first English Literature lesson 'easily' that term and so produced a number of poetry extracts suggested by the GCSE Exam Board for analysis. All the students had to do was go around the room and read the extracts on the different sheets. Everything, Jack would come to realise, was practical in Mr Hussein's classroom. Everything came from the GCSE Exam Board, whether on soft days like this one or over the course of dreary sessions on examination technique: how to structure sentences with embedded clauses (like calluses); how to introduce conflict into an argument; how to put your own spin on the subject within rigidly *specific* limits. Nothing was ever at all organic. Nothing was learnt but what was a necessity. The norm was passionless. It was efficient, dead.

That being said, once the other students had funnelled into the class and a particular blonde girl was tasked with reading a poem by the early modern poet John Donne, Jack began to understand what Mr Hussein and Basil's agreement might have been. He didn't know what to make of it. Nor did he expect researching the Alawite sect in more detail would clarify the matter. What was important was what he saw—and he saw a lot, scarcely any of it being previously imaginable. For, in the middle of the class, the blonde girl named Agatha Darger stood up to read, and he could instantly tell that Basil was in love.

> *Oh stay, three lives in one flea spare,*
> *Where we almost, nay more than married are.*
> *This flea is you and I, and this*
> *Our marriage bed, and marriage temple is;*

This was probably the point where Jack heard the sound of Basil's dropping his pen. A smudge on the page. Nobody else looked.

> *Though parents grudge, and you, w'are met,*
> *And cloistered in these living walls of jet.*
> *Though use make you apt to kill me,*
> *Let not to that, self-murder added be,*
> *And sacrilege, three sins in killing three.*

The poem was from the A Level syllabus and was called *The Flea*. 'Not to get ahead of ourselves!' Mr Hussein had said—although he, too, perhaps insufficiently sensitive to its innuendos before, asked Agatha to stop reading after the stanza above. Neither did he ask her to make a comment on the poem, as he had the other students, in case some unsightly interpretation of marriage or killing was dispersed amongst them that the few Wahabis in the class—Mahmud and Jamal—would doubtless enjoy.

Jack Grundon, however, had another theory about what was going on. He looked over to Basil, who had stopped his industrious writing or translating or whatever he was doing, and noticed the Syrian's wet eyes. He couldn't tell if he was correct or not about Basil's feelings for the girl. Then Jack studied Agatha more closely. So this was her. There was the missing tooth in the upper right corner of her mouth, the red birthmark on her neck. Piercingly, she looked directly back at him with her angry green eyes. He controlled himself. He switched his eyesight to a dove flying out the window. 'I wasn't thinking about anything, actually,' Jack told himself.

Now, Mr Hussein said, Jack had to read a poem by Louise Bennet-Coverley, which was then on the GCSE English syllabus. Later that month, on the London tube, Jack saw it printed above his seat in the train carriage. The poem, though his developing literary sensibilities practically made him allergic to it, was called *Colonisation in Reverse*, and he read it too enthusiastically to be taken seriously but just enthusiastically enough not to infuriate Mr Hussein or the cabal of Africans that sat directly behind him in almost every lesson. He had to do his best Jamaican accent without getting punched.

> *Wat a joyful news, miss Mattie,*
> *I feel like me heart gwine burs*
> *Jamaica people colonizin*
> *Englan in reverse.*

> *By de hundred, by de tousan*
> *From country and from town,*
> *By de ship-load, by de plane-load*
> *Jamaica is Englan boun.*

Perhaps it was the glowing red eyes of Jamal that made Mr Hussein permit Jack to skip to the last stanza rather than go through the whole thing; he and Agatha were paired in this. Yet Jack, for some reason, was on the verge of tears as he moronically read it. Even he did not expect himself to cry at something so stupid, so funny, if he were honest. But was it funny at all—if he were honest?

> *Wat a devilment a Englan!*
> *Dem face war an brave de worse,*
> *But me wonderin how dem gwine stan*
> *Colonizin in reverse.*

At this point, Jack sat down because his face was red and his nose had started streaming, and when he looked behind him,

Jamal was covering his face in his hands and cackling at the 'weak ass liddle white boy', before being sent out for adding the word 'faggot' on top of that. Five minutes later, it would be the end of the lesson; Jack looked at Agatha. Agatha smiled sympathetically for a second before the anger at him from before surged across her lips. There was also something else. It was weird, as was she. Jack felt a pulse deep inside the core of his head; it felt like water reverberating around a heavy stone submerged in the middle of a cave. And was he the stone or the water? Because her eyes were not just green, but so radically green he did not know what to make of them. They were sharp at the edges. Was she wearing makeup? What was the name of the film that started with a camera zooming into a big green eye with ambience in the background that sounded like the shifting of tectonic plates?

"rirnrnrnirnrinrinrr—"

The bell made him jump when it sounded. There were a few cackles. People started to leave, the back row lifting themselves up collectively like too many dark clothes being pulled up on one little coat hanger. A few tittered, drifted. A girl named Jemima ran her hand through a boy's dreadlocks, and he burped at her. When the boy left, her friends turned to her from the area behind their desks and said something that Jack didn't hear.

'Did you like my reading, yeah?' said a rough, light voice.

Jack tried to locate the source of the voice for a second. Surely it was somewhere out there, where the natural pairings of timid white girls and jockeying black boys made their combinations. He returned his sight to one place he had not allowed himself yet to look: back at Agatha.

'The flea,'—gravel gushed from her lips, or that's how she sounded.

'It was impressive,' Jack said, automatically. 'You're a natural.'

'—wants to climb up me.'

She said this without laughing or joking. Her stare lingered. It was the stare of something extraordinarily old and tired. Her eyes wobbled: these were exterminated and exterminating eyes.

'... What do you want me to say?' said Jack.

Agatha shrugged her shoulders. She inspected him curiously, the left side of his face. He bit his lip.

'... *Vir-gin* ...'

'What?'

She rolled her eyes, got her brown leather satchel, and stood up. She looked at him for a second more with a completely different attitude. Jack couldn't tell what it was. Then she vanished down the left corridor. Her steps were quick, heavy. The sound was of someone walking with a limp. Meanwhile, though Jack didn't see him, Basil Alawi was looking intently at Jack, then straight ahead of him, not leaving the class even during lunchtime. A crest of pale sweat dripped from the top of his hairline. He picked up his pen as Mr Hussein went on his laptop at the back of the class.

The one class that followed, Physics, was thankfully a video lesson during which a thirty-five-minute documentary on the formation of planets would be played. This was followed by ten minutes of 'funny' fifteen-second videos at the request of the students to keep them entertained. Then there were questions. Then a twelve-minute documentary was shown to explain the formula for calculating gravitational potential energy ... eventually.

Time passed. It passed Jack by.

As the school day ended and the final bell seemed to ring through the entire universe, Jack trudged along with so many others out towards the parking lot. He glanced up and over the school fence to see if his mother was there, but the sun emerged from behind the clouds, so he couldn't see. He turned back towards the gravel path out of the gate, where crowded luxury cars swarmed the pickup lane, cloaked parents inside pulling up to the school. Many of the cars were more expensive than he could imagine the fathers of most of the boys could afford. For Lamborghinis and Ferraris were there, even if the wealth that afforded them wasn't on display in the manners of those who drove them. As Jack left through the black gates and entered the street, he noticed a small rift in the sole of his left shoe. Maybe a stone had jammed in there earlier, and he hadn't managed to remove it in time. He felt a bit embarrassed and looked for a spot to wait.

But then the crowd bulged and absorbed him. He was caught in a mass of blazers, bikes, and balaclavas whirling into the sides of cars and down towards the shops. He felt as if he were going to be carried along by it, like a small bird caught amid the thunderous migration of a flock of geese. He was tall, but the impulses of so many suddenly to surge, split off, mob, or crash into, if it were felt to be necessary or exciting enough—*to crash into*, overwhelmed him. A girl was knocked over by the crowd, and it appeared to eat her. The blazers and black coats blazed over her, sealed over her like a winding fabric. She had wandered out at her own pace, and the crowd had spread its wings and talons over her. Jack saw and then did not see her. Wireless speakers pulsed from the back of backpacks, and faces cackled, shoved juice cartons into themselves, pulsed, pumped. She was being swept along. He elbowed and bumped to get back to the fence. He couldn't help but say 'Excuse me! Excuse me! Please let me through.' And then, they were gone, and he watched the shoving, jostling, crowd go around the corner.

The street was quiet. Jack could hear a wren's nervous chirps in the distance, as if its territory were under attack. He turned his mind towards what he was not meant to acknowledge had happened to him that afternoon. Some moisture accumulated in his right eye, and he remembered the humiliation of the day itself. Because what, *anyway*, was his next day at school actually going to be like? How would he manage the sheer misery of that poetry reading for the rest of the term now that nobody could forget he was such a crybaby? Even at an all-white school, his behaviour would have marked him out for torment. At his school, however, the stares of Jamal and his friends had locked on him like ... he couldn't quite recall the comparison. Why did it have to be so hard? *Who was Basil Alawi?* Jack promised himself to drop the topic. Yet when Mary Phillips arrived late at the school gates in her car, crammed as it was with pieces of furniture she had decided to purchase after Jack's father had persuaded her to give him back his old couch, Jack was already prepared for a political rant. He would tell his mother everything about how he was feeling because that way his all-powerful mother would at least be able, somehow, to do something to help him. Or maybe she would simply understand.

'But it can't be *all* bad!' Mary said, turning the wheel and staring at Jack to signal him to stop complaining as she went round the roundabout.

'But that's what's happening, Mum!' Jack said, red-faced. 'That's what's happening!'

'Jack Grundon, you are being a lunatic! Calm down if you want me to listen to you!'

Jack went quiet. The car went around. Mary drove a little longer than usual through the area by their house so that Jack could get his words out. She thought she understood the importance of letting him release his anger: it would probably be a nightmare at home later if he wasn't allowed at least a little grumble now.

Nonetheless, the part of himself that Jack considered shameful, victim of everything, responsible for nothing, theorised and orated relentlessly to Mary for fifteen minutes as they passed a grey-haired mother putting her washing-up out to dry, two women in niqabs that looked like the wives of the same short sixty-year-old man sneering behind them, a church made mostly of flint with graffiti on its outside saying something incomprehensible, the war memorial where he and Mary had seen the drunk Arab sit. No one was there now.

They arrived at their house. Whatever Jack had said, and however inarticulately, caused Mary Phillips to pull the keys out of the car, leave the furniture and Jack inside it, and go out and walk in the area of the garden around where Betty and Betsy had once lived and daisies spread now. Jack sat by himself. He had sweat all over his forehead. Jack covered his face in his hands and blew his nose on the tissues that were there. Mary Phillips thought about telephoning his father, blaming his pro-Brexit attitudes for *his* son's racism, then thought of doing what the TV recommended, the chimera with the red, bleeding mouth, which was reporting Jack to Prevent.

Prevent was a noble agency; it was the government department where the good guys worked to fight fascism, apparently, and that's why the TV described them in that way. They were meant to deal with extreme sentiments like Jack's, diagnose them, if necessary. Mary Phillips recalled that her friends had—two of them—got their sons diagnosed with autism and got them on Ritalin as soon as they required. But having heard Jack's logical-emotional cries, Mary did not know about making a similar trip to Prevent (which she *personally* thought of as a hybrid of the police and the psychiatrist's office). Ultimately, Mary supposed that she was old-fashioned, and that that, probably, was part of the problem. She shrugged off her shoes and grounded herself in the grass, thinking of everything she had raised Jack on: *Jerusalem*, *Narnia*. And his father had made him trawl through *Notes from Underground*. Perhaps that was all. Every other poem and book emanated from those three. So, what else could it be? Maybe it was the iPad that made Jack think in the way that he did, its videos of hideous, intolerant mobs. Even if they *were* real, those foreign hordes, in

Italy and Slovakia and Germany and Ireland and France, they needn't be shown to a boy. For what would the world come to if they were shown ... as they were?

Mary Phillips looked down over the sunset burning away behind the grass, which rustled as the light sifted through the leaves, looked to her phone, the number in the ever-growing dark.

She did not call it then but might have. For all the world, she might have! Her fingers hesitated over the button before she shut the phone off. It would have been so easy. Report your son for being a thought-criminal, but in a Liberal Democracy, so it's good; it's moral! Report your son to Prevent. *All is well, and you are good! The state loves you! You are an intellectual! Have a TV interview!* Yes, that was easy. Being on the side of power was always easy. But being on the side of her son, she concluded, that was not, although that was also love. So to herself she concluded and to God she promised, she must be on his side. She would be.

Yet as soon as she had reached the end of this thought process, Mary noticed how bizarre it was. Why was she having *this* reaction to Jack's silly comments? She was reacting like Jack had raped a girl! Mary hated that word, even thinking of it and saying it offended her. But that was surely the only thing deserving of the awful, stigmatic terror in her brain. What else could force her to report her baby? Perhaps in that moment, she had her own dream of the bloody red chimera's gnashing mouth, rejected it, remembered the desecrated war memorial. Probably not.

Meanwhile, in the car, Jack opened his phone—saw that Telegram, the app that Basil had asked him to install, had received two messages. There was one from Basil and one from another source. Basil's contact just displayed his picture. But the other person who had messaged Jack had the avatar of a anthropomorphic cartoon cat with bags under her eyes and a loose-fitting top. He checked; the account's name was AgathaD914. Jack felt his head, rubbed it, and thought about what was coming, what could possibly come up, the worst thing. Before opening her message, he looked to Basil Alawi's and saw the brazen column of thoughts that he had sent.

This time, I'm going to forgive you for looking at her as you did.
She's a sexy girl, that can't be denied.
Yet she doesn't concern you as you think she does.
Whatever you do, don't get in the way or try and get in the way.
I do, in fact, regard you as my friend and I think we could be useful to each other.
But, at the end of the day, I know what I want.
That's Agatha.
And if you have any disagreements about my union with her, which if I were a white man then I would have, address me as an Arab, which is what I am.
If not, by helping me facilitate this relationship, you will win yourself my eternal friendship.
I can open doors for you. But that is enough for this evening.

Basil deleted this message almost immediately after Jack had read it. He was suddenly online, and then Jack was blocked and unable to contact Basil ever again.

In that moment, how was Jack meant to describe what he felt? The message was alien. It was from another planet, and it exposed that between him and someone he believed himself capable of befriending, there really were hundreds, if not thousands, of years of separation. Yes, Basil had written it in Jack's language, but behind it lurked an entirely different spirit. It was obvious that Basil and he, now and forever, were different, absolutely different. Incredible that it had taken him so long to notice! But it was true. There was nothing in what Basil had written that he could identify with, and, in truth, despite liking his English clothes and accent, Basil probably felt exactly the same way about Jack. For though he dressed and spoke like an Englishman, Basil wrote like—(Jack searched for the comparison)—a mafia member. He used the tone of a criminal ashamed of having been sniffed out. Jack wondered if he would be capable of it, that kind of language, that amoral bargaining, even if he ended up breaking the law. Basil's tribalism was so foreign to him that he decided not.

Then Jack went to Agatha's message as the sun died under the horizon. It was terse and simple, rude to him, and yet he understood it.

I did not like the way you lookd at me, and we need to talk.

FOUR

But it was many months before Agatha would confront Jack, and in that time, he was exposed to nothing and everything. He had gone in and out of over one hundred lessons. He had looked searchingly at Basil and held back his stare from Agatha in Mr Hussein's English class. He had performed presentations on the Indian region of Kerala for Geography that bored him to tears. He had been forced into going to an after-school street-dance class by his mother when she realised he wasn't making many friends, because that, apparently, was how you made them. He had turned fifteen without applause. He had prayed insincerely in the chapel before the young vicar Oliver Turner, and he had prayed sincerely by himself after having a sequence of nightmares about death. In one of these, Jack had seen himself in a glass coffin thousands of miles under the Earth. This coffin, Jack's coffin, had no air in it. Meanwhile, if he looked out into the void, he could see dozens of other people luxuriating in their expansive glass tombs that were filled with oxygen and, for some symbolic reason, red petals. In the largest one of these was Basil, always Basil. He was snoring in a temple carved out of ice. Jack felt that this was a dream about not being liked and finding out that the only intelligent person worth speaking to had grown almost inevitably into a stranger. Last but not least, Jack had been taken to a psychiatrist recommended by the school after getting into an altercation with Muhammad Akbar, who had torn up Jack's tattered copy of *As I Lay Dying*, when he had dared to say that there was no Allah whatsoever and probably no God at all. The psychiatry session had been brief and coddling. It had taken place in an office that was as pale, empty, and serene as any part of Jack's increasingly non-white school. As for the psychiatrist, she was a Nigerian woman named Mia with a posh English accent. Her office was decorated with images of black figures and 'secular saints' (Sigmund Freud, Angela Davis) gesturing with their hands in the air alongside slogans like 'Unlock Your Inner Power'.

As for the discussion, it started and ended when Jack said he didn't feel wholly responsible for the incident with Muhammad. He wasn't allowed to say anything more than he had given himself the opportunity to say, meaning talking or shouting over Mia, who had already 'read everything' about the incident. She knew what was what, she said, and she felt it might even be advisable to read one of her favourite quotations about healing from Bell Hooks, an author whose name you always apparently have to spell in the lower case. The quotation that Mia read was: 'To know love we have to invest time and commitment.' Mia liked this a lot. She showed Jack the line on the A-Z Quotes website and asked him to read it aloud. Jack said: 'Wow.'

Jack would have to learn about love, Mia noted. Jack would need to love Muhammad and, Mia insinuated, make up for the colonial sins of his forefathers. Jack was about to say something, but she refused to allow him to speak, and then when he started talking about how alienated he felt in these classrooms surrounded by—'*No offence!*'—violent people, she asked him what exactly had made him feel that way, considering all the while the possibility that he had been radicalised by the Far Right or if this was not already an incurable National Socialist before her, just telling her 'the truth', as he whitely saw it? Either way, Mia did not like being disagreed with and regarded being questioned in this manner as representing the air of some disorder in Jack. He was promptly, affectionately prescribed antidepressants, and Mia said something to him about softening down the rough edges that he, Jack, had artificially constructed between his true self, which wanted to love, and the others that surrounded him in the world, who also wanted to love and were just like him. And he would realise this, Mia said smilingly, if he just thought about it.

Then Mary Phillips was invited into the room, and despite her instinctive dislike of everything that this woman had said to her before the session, despite her growing distrust of experts and the media that started during Lockdown, she nodded along. Even though a Moroccan man had followed her that morning down the street with hungry lips, even though she always carried mace now that she had found a supplier, illegal as it was, and so carrying mace made her, like Jack, something of a rebel, she agreed with Mia. With whatever residual belief she still had in the state, the school, the idea that there is no such thing as race, and if there is, we must not speak about it, she accepted what was going to happen. For if she did speak about race, what would become of her? She would be an enemy of the state and everybody, and so would her son if he continued down this path. She loved her son. And so out of love, Jack was prescribed Cipralex. They queued and purchased the harmless-looking tablets from a nearby chemist. They went home. Jack wasn't to tell his father about them, but Mary said that she would in time.

Within a week, Jack was staring at the pill bottle in the school cafeteria and reading the word 'E-s-c-i-t-a-l-o-p-r-a-m' repeatedly inside his head, the name of the drug, having already swallowed his first dose that morning. He was hyper-functional and numb. He was not angry. He tolerated everything that happened around him and sometimes, but only sometimes, raised his hand in lessons. If he could describe the feeling, not that he felt any particular need to whatsoever, filling up his frontal lobe, he would call it blandness. The medicine filled him with blandness. He told his mother how the tablets made him feel one day, and she said that blandness was better than depression. But, sitting there in the canteen, Jack felt like a cartoon character, drawn on the side of a steamed-up window, who had just had his face wiped off. That was his first reaction to escitalopram. He also felt an area near the back of his skull throb every so often, not that it bothered him. What bothered him was how the medicine affected his inner life, how his imagination worked. Only two and a half years ago, he had dreamed constantly of a maverick boy who looked like himself and a cybernetic hound raiding an enormous Mesoamerican temple for gold and princesses with eyes of jade and wings of daffodils blooming from their backs.

Not anymore: rarely now did inspiration strike him as it used to. He could describe things well. But the tablets effectively eradicated the thrill of the unexpected. Inside him, there was a pale flood of fluid circulating and drowning the world in his brain, suffocating and burying and petrifying his adventurers, like a volcano's pyroclastic flow. Jack imagined, because it was one of the few things he could easily imagine, a totally featureless building enmeshed with clouds. Occasionally, there was mood lighting. Blues and relaxing greens were projected onto its face. But there was nothing ever there now that could distract him from producing answers to the four- and six-mark questions set before him during the first round of exams. He received in Physics, Biology, and Chemistry some of the highest marks in the year and was totally unbothered by the happy news of this he heard from his mother when she got an email about it from the school. Agatha gazed at him every so often in English lessons. His father treated him to a meal at an expensive restaurant and drank three glasses of wine in his son's name.

Jack Grundon supposed that he was pleased.

He had learnt the secret to getting 28 marks out of 30 on every essay question he could be asked about the play *An Inspector Calls* that they were studying in English for GCSEs. The secret was being numb to all aspects of the play that were intriguing outside of the proscribed mark scheme—for instance, the fact that it was initially performed in Leningrad—and constantly taking the pharmaceuticals that were necessary for doing that at all. His head was a mechanical factory in which the workers did not ask questions. The product of the factory was success.

At the end of Mr Miles's Physics class on a Wednesday in April, Jack was asked to stay behind with another 'top student' from class 11B, again a little older than Jack, whom the school intended to potentially send with him to Cambridge University on a long enough timeline. This was Frederick, or as he called himself, 'Fauna'—naming himself after a character from Hololive, whatever that was. He was perhaps the tallest boy Jack had encountered in the school, although his painful slouch over the blue desks of the Physics room was so abhorrent, thought Jack immediately, that it needed to be bent back into shape by tongs and screws and hammers and other tools. This was not a complete person. This was an intellect plus a body that it dragged behind itself like a badly broken umbrella. But why was Jack having these thoughts? Why did he dislike someone as wise and nervous as himself, but transgender and covered in deep scars? 'Oh, that's why,' thought Jack, shaking Fauna's hand, which felt like a knotty tangle of reeds.

'Pleased to meet you,' said Fauna, grinning.

'Pleased to meet you,' said Jack, feeling a little more than bland numbness.

They sat down adjacent to one another, lowering into their chairs at almost the same angle and with the same timing. Fauna even looked in the other direction when Jack turned his head round to confront him, before presciently imitating Jack's outraged head-turn to the right, back at Fauna, grinding his teeth. It was revolting; Jack had never imagined either imitation or geometry to be revolting before, but now that it was it could be always. Fauna was copying him flirtatiously.

'So-ree ...' Fauna laughed with phlegm in his nostrils.

'Why?' said Jack. 'Why?'

Fauna scanned Jack out of the corner of his left eye, the one with the bigger painted eyelashes than on the right. Fauna felt the corners of his mouth, perhaps questioning whether or not it would be more appropriate to wear a face mask over his bulbous chin today, gauging Jack's reaction, before producing just such a face mask, pink, from his purse, and then putting it away all over again as soon as Jack noticed the letters 'UwU' inscribed on its front, and cleared his throat instinctively.

'You seem disturbed. So I'm so-ree,' said Fauna.

'Are you dragging out your sorry on purpose?'

'So-ree,' said Fauna, deliberately creeping to a higher intonation.

His hand with pink-painted nails patted Jack on the shoulder, and Jack's whole body shivered before Fauna went back to his laptop, which he was allowed to use for some reason. Jack turned his own way to face Mr Miles and felt very glad that a grey bar separated their legs under the table. The lesson began.

If the purpose of these additional tutorial sessions was to make sure that both candidates, Jack and Fauna, passed their GCSEs with flying colours and then prepared them for their A Levels, they might have been considered somewhat useful. To the extent that they were not useful, Jack Grundon was made to interact with Fauna Williams. When they sat next to each other in front of Mr Miles and Fauna would talk about the etymology of planet names and sprinkle in Platonic philosophy

whenever he could and mention the bizarre atomic consequences of quantum entanglement—particles that share the
same fate no matter how far apart—Jack could often do little
more than stare at Fauna's body. He was shocked at what it had
become. He was looking at a man in a custom-made school-
girl uniform that was at least two sizes too small, with arms of
different lengths, hairy wrists, and almost definitely a severely
receding hairline under his black wig. The less Jack thought
about the other parts of Fauna's body, the better.

But Fauna didn't think about Jack as Jack thought about
Fauna. Whereas Jack wanted to rip Fauna's eyes out every time
they lingered a little too long between his legs, Fauna wanted
to give his eyes to Jack for nothing at all, tear them out—and
would give chunks of his own brain also if Jack would only ask
for them. Because Fauna was fascinated by Jack. Fauna looked
at this boy, this bright-eyed, frightened young thing, and
thought about how he had been exposed to the same process
that he himself had: the same breaking down of masculine self-
hood, the same accelerated spiritual disintegration at the end
of a European culture, the same lack of mentorship, the same
(perhaps?) redistribution of wrist flesh into scars that smiled
and cackled at having asserted themselves. All this, Fauna pre-
sumed, Jack had been through; it was a very selfish sympathy,
but a kind of strange sympathy, nonetheless. Fauna considered
Jack to be three-quarters the same as himself. Yet Jack had his
holdout. Jack had his ignorance, his even greater youth. Fauna
wanted to turn Jack into what he, Fauna, had been turned.
From this desire, his affection for Jack sprung.

In the email chats that they were recommended to have, and which a few of them Jack did contribute to, Fauna talked constantly about the philosopher René Descartes and, whether or not Fauna had actually read him, the separation of the mind from the body. Fauna said that there was 'an aristocracy' to this, to the idea that mortal flesh was a prison and should be stripped away from the fabric of the soul, which ought to be free, but wasn't. Fauna spoke of artificial intelligence and industrialisation, of the sprouting forth of man as a flower from the ground, intent on abandoning his prior nature, his roots. The male form, Fauna thought, and very often said, was disgusting. There was nothing aesthetic about it. It was a shambling mass of dysgenic mutations. He decided to send Valerie Solanas's *The S.C.U.M Manifesto*, a book by a geneticist turned feminist. The acronym stood for 'Society for Cutting Up Men', Fauna explained.

In another email chain, Fauna sent Jack and then after class tried to read him *The Transmaxxing Manifesto*. In reply, Jack had simply written: 'What the fuck.' This was a book that argued, based on rigorous statistical analysis, the impossibility of having a satisfying life as a man in the twenty-first century. It concerned the acidic effect of dating apps on 'romantic markets'. It concerned pair-bonds and the breakdown of women's attachment to those who would have been, in other times, their first loves. It concerned the additional oxytocin recognised to be produced in unattractive men after they had been through various transgender surgeries, implanting plastics into their chests and shooting oestrogens into their arms and thighs. It recognised the importance of what was called 'the pink vortex' and stepping out of the male body, perhaps as members of the legendary Cathar sect strove to step out of the world, Fauna added. It was mad stuff. But Fauna believed it because Fauna had to believe in it.

Despite being a 'transwoman', or probably because of it, Fauna was the man that Jack had heard the most about the nature of women from. Having neither had much interest in women beforehand, nor now, having heard all of this, really wanting to build up more of an interest than he had already, Jack studied what Mr Miles wanted and nothing more. Fauna continued to insist on these discussions. But Jack studied. After four and a half weeks, nothing had altered. Fauna sent messages. Jack read some but not all of Fauna's messages. Jack worked extremely hard. They did not get on.

One day, behind the blinds in Mr Miles's Physics classroom, the sun seemed to pulse and fade as if instructing Jack to hurry up and finish the practice exam paper he was attempting. Jack filled in the last question and thought to himself that the reason he had bothered speaking to one he instinctively disliked as much as Fauna was that Fauna was the kind of man who could have been his mentor in another age; he was so intelligent, so much smarter than Jack—*smarter than Basil?*—it couldn't be denied. Yet Fauna had been stripped not only of any dignity that he possessed but any dignity that he could possess in the future. He had stripped himself. It was gone. He was still male, but now he couldn't grow up, mature, become an initiated man. Hormone blockers had taken care of that, however lately applied. And as for Fauna's mind, his thoughts ... they were gaping wounds. They were blood. They were hunger for blood and hatred of flesh and horror at Being; Jack began to notice Fauna's looking over at him as something to be remade and remade badly.

This was the catalyst for a change in Jack's life. For that Saturday evening, sitting at his father's desk in his flat as the man went on one of his inchoate rants about Tucker Carlson and reading an article about the bioethics of suicide that Fauna had sent him, Jack tried to give up his interest in philosophy forever. Clearly, philosophy had done something to Fauna. What had happened to Fauna could easily happen to him, and what the process had entailed must have been akin to a gradual demonic possession. Because it wasn't like, or it didn't use to be like, parents just one day decided to give in to the delusional requests of their son for surgeries and injections that would almost certainly ruin his life. That's at least what Jack thought.

No, he concluded, first the parents had to be whittled down by the TV. Maybe Fauna also helped whittle them down, that theologian and that professor of law, apparently, using their humanitarian principles against them, expanding the causes they recognised to include a new struggle that had lived under their roof, right next to them all along! This would have paralleled Fauna's own whittling down when faced with the poison of internet addiction, the fact of his country's demographic replacement, the endless stream of propaganda that encouraged him to do away with heterosexuality in the wake of #Metoo, even and perhaps especially as a young boy destined to repeat the mistakes of the past unless cleansed of all *so-called* natural inclinations. Jack had already been through all that. And so had Fauna. But what Fauna had done, Jack felt (and saw in Fauna's tiny, wriggling face) was to give in to the lie. Fauna had allowed himself to be destroyed, or at least that's what Jack supposed, and all that was left was a wastrel—his mutilated mentor.

Yet it hadn't been destruction without cause. Little did Jack know that at another time in Fauna's life, Fauna had been relentlessly bullied by his sister, and this culminated in Fauna's, then Frederick, being accused of doing something unclear to her and that she had deliberately made it unclear (because the sister in question did not want to acknowledge that a thirteen-year-old boy she had been babysitting had gotten her pregnant). As always, Fauna's parents sided with her. Then Fauna was almost imprisoned and given a 'caution'. Then, instead of prison, it was off to a therapist like Mia for him, one eager to diagnose those she saw as deserving treatment like punishment. Fauna was put on antidepressants. Then it was on to YouTube for him. Then it was on to ContraPoints. Then it was on to pornography. And then, soon enough, a desire to extinguish the masculine was born; to have done with providing for women, who hated you as a man; to have done with work and labour. At last, Fauna had concluded after a life of pointless suffering that it was his turn to *get* things for being attractive. And if he couldn't have that, then he would accept the social position that would compel others, his sister included, to respect his self-conscious mockery of them and his desire to possess a beauty that he could not. The TV made this much easier than any historian of a future age would suppose possible. Fauna had decided to live by its rules. As a result, he had become distorted as a figure within a flickering, dying screen.

'Goodbye, philosophy,' Jack thought.

Jack turned from his laptop, from the article from Fauna that tried to link the suicide of macrobacteria with Spartan eugenic breeding practices and those to the idea that unsuccessful, ugly, or mentally unstable modern individuals ought to embrace alternate or transgender lifestyles to prevent their seed from going on, and looked at his father. Jack looked around the room. He got out of his head. He saw the crumbs on the floor where bagatelles had been eaten. He saw the grey carpet. The room was about seventy square metres. There was a bed that was convertible into a couch; there was also his dad's old couch. Over the walls by it were two bookcases containing collections of poetry in no particular order and more than one biography of Philip Larkin. There were stains adjacent to the desk at which Jack sat.

Jack turned and studied his father's face, the tufts of grey hair all over his head, the long, vulture-like nose, the wobbling, dribbling double chin that always looked like it wanted to get something out. In spite of all of this, his father was an attractive man. He looked like a Roman bust, but attached to a base of withering limbs. He talked sometimes in an almost Irish accent. But most of the time he mumbled. He sounded like cosmic background radiation, the swishing of infinite empty static noise, in comparison to Fauna's ultra-precise transmissions of life-ruining nonsense. If he were serious, Jack couldn't tolerate either of them anymore—but especially Fauna's method of expressing himself.

'No,' he told himself, 'no. In truth, there is what is, and there is what is not.' There were the crumbs in his hands when he gathered them from under the placemat on the desk; there were his hands; there was his laptop. There was the window cut out of the same blank, pictureless white walls as he seemed to find everywhere else in the world. These were real, and the white walls were especially real. Enough philosophy and rambling: *how about white walls?* At school, the white walls stretched themselves through the cafeteria, his form room near the Design and Technology Department, Mr Miles's Physics classroom, Mr Tomlinson's Maths classroom, although that had a red ceiling, through Mr Hussein's English classroom, finishing in the Physical Education Hall. It was all the same, a school made in the stamp of those controllers who overtook Britain following the Second World War, at which time it supposedly became fashionable to make everything identical, to efface difference. Whiteness effaced. Then whiteness was effaced.

At this point in his meditation, Jack quickly realised he couldn't entirely do without philosophy, or some understanding of the ideas that secretly ruled the world. For they *so* ruled it that much of their influence went totally unobserved by men like his father, who prided themselves on being intellectuals. What was it that the young vicar Oliver Turner had mentioned during the last school visit to St Michael's? It overlapped with what he was currently thinking.

Jack pulled the front of his hair and tried to concentrate as his father decided to tell him about the significance of David Bowie, although Jack, who only liked ambient tracks, didn't appreciate him as much. What was it the young vicar had said? Turner had mentioned a Bible verse concerning powers, concerning 'The Powers'—Jack looked it up and found it, briefly mourned that the computer was dulling the strand in his memory that would have allowed him to recall the reference on his own. Jack said the lines to himself quietly enough that they overrode the distraction of his father without alerting him that he wasn't paying attention.

Oliver Turner, the young vicar, had told him on the day of the school trip, perhaps solely in order to impress him, a verse from the Epistle to the Ephesians. Turner was a sad-faced, long-necked, man of middling height with a long red moustache, and sometimes a flat cap. He belonged to the Church of England, and you wouldn't think him a priest, because he belonged to the Church of England. That day, sitting with a coffee cup between his legs in one of the pews of St Michael's, and studying Jack as he gazed at the stained-glass window with the big muscular angel in it, Oliver Turner had asked him what the matter was because Jack looked sad.

Jack had said: 'What is it all there for?'

And he had said: 'The glass? That's mainly for decoration.'

'I mean spiritual healing. I mean Jesus. What is it all there for?'

'Ah.'

'So what is it all there for?'

'Well ...'

'—*What is it all there for?*'

'I suppose,' sighed Oliver Turner. 'You're at the age where asking *why* over and over to an adult who can't answer you makes you feel clever.' Oliver Turner wiped his mouth and thought. 'The reason we have Jesus is—' and he paused to remember Ephesians 6:12.

'Yes?' said Jack, very quietly.

'For we wrestle not against flesh and blood, but against principalities, against powers, against the rulers of the darkness of this world, against spiritual wickedness in high places.'

That was something. Yes, but what did that *something* mean? From hearing the lines from Ephesians, Jack had immediately turned outside—to the white light through the door, to where Basil, he imagined, had been standing with the other Muslims whilst he had toured the font, browsed through a Book of Common Prayer, met the priest. But had it been Basil? The figure standing there had seemed larger, though Basil was near, lingering behind perhaps. No matter.

Jack, remembering all of this at his father's desk, let his hair go. He was back in the present moment. Now, he heard the sounds of his father again: some analysis of the song 'Life on Mars', a question about Fauna's bioethics article that was totally unrelated to it, the throat-slashing sound of a wine bottle's being opened. But Jack didn't presently care what the man said or did because what Oliver Turner had said that day at St Michael's had been true. They were, indeed, ruled by principalities, by powers that tolerated the bullying and intimidation of some—who, even, sometimes themselves joined in with

it—and had others arrested merely for complaining about it.
Jack knew that a migrant could grope a woman on the train
and face no prison time; he had learnt this, awfully, in his
mother's case. But an Englishman photographing it might get
two years. This wasn't just government tyranny. This was an
ethical system behind a government system that was flat-out
cancerous. Who had come up with it? Maybe, thought Jack,
the powers that Oliver Turner had spoken about.

Jack had little interest in the theological, or so he told himself. Yet what but some evil spirit could have led to the absurd
world before him? It was a political theology, he told himself,
that had created this world. He gazed out of the window as the
sun went down, scowling, and guessed he looked ridiculous,
which he probably did, as his father started babbling about the
Philip Larkin poem "Church Going" to nobody at all, 'How a
man doesn't know what he has until it's too late!'

Tired of taking his unnecessary medication, maybe also of
the limitless praise he received for his grades (but not all too
much), Jack decided to avoid taking Cipralex for a day or two.
For one of these days, his inner sense of bland numbness lingered. He thought about the noise of his father at the back
of the room and found himself as distracted as he could have
possibly been by it. The most notable thing he saw that day
was another boy called Muhammad, whom he had met once,
punching a fat Indian boy in the back of the head over and over
again on the basketball pitch on the same road as his father's
flat. Then Jack had gone back to his mother's house, seen his
mother, and fallen asleep almost immediately. It had been 4

p.m., and it had been raining. For some reason, coming off the tablets had made him react more than taking them in the first place. Jack slept all the way through the night as it rained and did not dream. He woke up five minutes late for school the next day and rushed his egg sandwich breakfast down his gullet. He left feeling a little sick.

It was on this second day of what could only be classified as withdrawal that he saw Agatha Darger again. How long had it been? He saw her on the walk to school, down what remained of the cobblestone pavement there. He was a little late, and he could tell just from the emptiness of the street, its noiselessness, that the dark crowd must have already entered the school. Just a few bikes whizzed by, and when he reached the final stretch, some seven minutes away from the front entrance, he glimpsed the back of her head. She held her satchel with a partly extended arm that nearly hit a lorry as it passed her on her left. She ran her other hand over the leaves on a house's white wall.

Once more, a pulse reverberated in Jack's head. She was walking very slowly. He planned to skitter by and overtake her, walking onto the left side of the road and going around where she had come to a standstill on the pavement. Weren't gentlemen supposed to walk on the far side of the road so that women didn't get splashed by puddles? One of her legs vibrated, quivered. It was as if there were a bug in her sock that she couldn't get out. Jack increased his pace, put his headphones on, and tuned into ambient noise. To the right of Agatha was a big steel gate, and beyond it was a quite extensive field, its grass wet with the rain of the last night. As planned, he stepped past her, but perhaps just slower than he had intended. Mesmerised by the field, he forgot for a second that Agatha was directly opposite him and that he had basically walked in front of her. But he didn't see Agatha's face when she stumbled and lunged. The field glowed. She took him by the collar of his blazer, yelled, 'WHERE WERE YOU?!' and, before he could answer, slapped him. She slapped him, and then she muttered her way through the steel gate into the field.

It happened so fast. He angrily felt his face.

'—WHERE WERE YOU!!—' she said even more loudly, back at him. Her teeth gnashed; he had never seen that before.

He watched her go. Agatha had always walked fast; she was known for her performance on the track team. But today she was far slower than any mere athletic sprain could make her. And so Jack, despite her best efforts, easily caught up with her. He followed her in. As he approached her, Jack noticed a red stain on the back of her sleeve, terror in her jaw, deep bags under her eyes. What was going on then? He had been smacked just softly enough to feel like he was the scapegoat for someone else. Jack looked down and noticed his shoes were soaked.

But now Agatha was moving, strenuously limping, and then she was all of a sudden at the other end of the field, about two hundred metres in front of him. *What was Jack's time, again, on the two hundred metres?* At that age, that, bizarrely, was what he immediately thought of. Yet as Agatha leant against the green bars at the other end of the field, which blended into the trees behind them, Jack knew she was waiting for him. She had

been willing to wait, had been betrayed—somehow, by him—
and yet was still willing to wait. The sun was incinerating.

Jack felt like putting down his bags and just raging, just
screaming after her for hitting him. But that was only half
of what was going on. Jack was also developing a deep and
increasingly total awareness of an almost, dare he say it, chi-
valric duty that he had neglected? Something, he had known,
had been going on between Agatha and Basil under his nose.
Already, he had stopped considering Basil a friend at the end of
his second term. Yet something else remained to be sorted out.
He thought about Bothelford's destroyed druidic cave, which
he and his mother had visited long ago, how the dynamite of
miners had, he felt, effaced a secret wanting to be revealed.

To Agatha, he would walk but not run. He would cradle his
sports bag, he would show her what he was made of, show this
idiot girl. He gritted his teeth and stomped; the uniform and
backpack filled with textbooks clambering over his spine like
a hefty tortoise shell. From a distance, he could tell there was
another tone in her face, a different 'theme', that was the best
word he could think of for it, that wanted to display itself. And
so he trotted on.

The grass of the field was partly wet and partly dry, partly
green and partly burned by the sun. It wasn't clean like it
looked from beyond the gate. There were bits of rubbish in
it, and there were no bins in sight, an oversight by the parish
council. Jack almost thought of 'trash' instead of 'rubbish', and
wondered how American his mind had become through media
exposure to the point where he had let that linguistic tendency

in. And then he forgot about it. In the distance, Agatha was sliding ever so slightly down and then up the bars she opposed. She was neither crying nor laughing. Whatever wanted to come out of her was desperate, urging itself forth, and perhaps had wanted to break loose for an all too painful period that he, Jack, was partly responsible for extending. Who cared about Fauna? Who cared about philosophy, his father?

Halfway through the field, Jack decided to chuck his bags and blazer down and go over to Agatha, speak to her, make it quick. There were many things he was prepared to hear well before his age, and perhaps this too would be one. He would be prepared.

Then, closing in on the stretched, horrifying face, alert with the sensation of a thousand years, he didn't know. But as he spoke to her, and she began to speak, he knew.

FIVE

'Here,' said Agatha. 'Here.'

As Jack approached her, he saw the true extent of how much she had changed. Her hair was long but, Jack thought, partly sheared, as though some huge monster had decided to take a clump off for his own purposes. Her eyes did not line up symmetrically, or didn't any longer. Her wrists seemed to turn in the wind, so light were they. She wore a satanic pin on the inside of her jacket, some juvenile protest against God or the gift of a sister who enjoyed Metal music, Jack didn't know. What he was confronted with was not a young girl but a kind of alabaster twitching doll. Awaiting him, what she was going to say, she gnashed behind her teeth. She gnashed her teeth till her jaw jutted as if it were glitching out of her face in a video game, and Jack instinctively scratched his own jaw in response.

He reached her, this twitching, stick-brained doll with eyes of porcelain—they seemed to stare absolutely nowhere, and wondered what he had gotten himself into. It wasn't good. Dared he put this down to her having an agonising period? He had heard about those. Those could be terrible. Or dared he try to contain the situation by asking a selfish question?

He would do that. That at least was decisive. He was blushing uncontrollably. He did neither; he spluttered.

'I'm not in love with you,' Jack said and shivered.

But Agatha was whispering some odd half-song off her mother's radio. Agatha breathed in heavily, exhaling as though her airways wanted to close off entirely if they only could. The drowsy fisheyes turned on him. She began, no, never started to laugh. She just breathed a tone, major.

'I do not give a fuck about you,' said Agatha, selflessly, and breathed. 'Yeah, yes.'

Jack hiccupped and did not even know what he was dealing with here.

Agatha looked up at the clouds, straining, as if she were trying to see behind them some zeppelin, some alien ship.

'How fucking much do you even know about fucking?' Agatha grinned.

This wasn't a child, thought Jack. This was someone between a retarded infant and a collapsing grandmother. He wondered whether she had always been like this, then remembered that she hadn't been, four or five months ago, or however long ago it was. She hadn't been. He had been on his Cipralex; he was blushing. He had been debating the meaning of life with Fauna and gotten his grades back. In that time, what had happened to her?

'How fucking much do you even know about fucking—' she repeated. It wasn't a question this time. How old even was this girl? Jack wondered whether he or she was older, or had he gotten younger, or had she gotten older? Jack had never heard such sincere swearing coming out of a fifteen-year-old girl. This was different from the swearing of immature boys like him. This was swearing with the full thrust of understanding. ... *What*, then, had happened to Agatha? What had he, Jack, allowed to happen, if he even permitted himself that responsibility?

Agatha lowered her asymmetrical gaze till at least one of her eyes, with a pupil that looked like it wanted to split into two, into frogspawn, met his face, his lips, his head. 'Suck ...' she said.

'What?' Jack said and closed his eyes a little longer than he wanted to. He felt rooted to the ground. He couldn't move.

Agatha's little hands, decorated with scissor cuts, they looked like, went up to her mouth. She peeled her lips back to show her gums like she was pulling a funny face in nursery. She was behaving like a three-year-old. 'Suck,' she said, and showed Jack her missing tooth, the swarming, mangled, blue, bruised gum around it.

Jack felt the air being pulled out of his lungs. The sting of the blow she had made to his face was nothing now. What kind of blue was that? What kind of purple? Jack recalled the first dissection class he had had in Biology and the electrified viscera of dead frogs.

'You see? Knows nothing,' said Agatha, flopping the lip back, veiling it, then swinging her arms a little. She leaned back against the bars and stood up taller. Whatever cloud had temporarily blocked the sun was pierced by a bright bolt of light that ignited the hidden flaming tones in her hair. Jack didn't know what it reminded him of, but a distant dream of Orpington feathers and wounds came into his mind. He would try to focus on that instead of the situation at hand. But then Agatha, Agatha who wasn't crowned by the sunlight at all because her crazy tortured face was a waxwork mannequin's even in the light, decided to ask him, 'Do you know who is in love with me ... fucking Jack, *fuck*-ing coward, would you like to know? Would you?'

Jack was beginning to get pictures in his head. Images of things he had seen before but hadn't had the context to process. He thought about the stubble on Basil's face, Basil's dreams about marrying a white wife, Basil dropping his pen on hearing a line from a poem about a marriage bed cloistered in living walls of jet; Basil's message describing Agatha as a 'sexy girl', and the fact that Jack, even at his new school's Parents' Evening, had never seen Basil's parents, not even once. Was Basil ... a grown-up masquerading as a student to—*the word found its way into his vocabulary from Agatha*—fuck? But how would that even work? 'Basil Alawi is a Muslim paedophile, my friend Basil Alawi, or who used to be my friend, is a Muslim paedophile ...' Jack thought. He couldn't think. It was stupid. It was so stupid. Was it possible?

As though a black sludge had entered the centre of his world, Jack looked over Agatha's slightly twitching form and superimposed, in his imagination, the image of the black man grinning and having sex with the white woman that Miss Wright had showed him in reception out of a book on gender expression, hated himself as he did it, felt, nevertheless, that he couldn't but do it. Was this what Miss Wright's lesson had been for? Was this, he thought, what frankly all those lessons about diversity, equity, and inclusion had been, all along, for? For enabling what had happened to Agatha; for conjuring forth images in his brain that naturalised what had happened to Agatha, like it was just something normal?

Agatha was playing with her wound again but seemed this time to be on the verge of crying her eyes out. There was no consistent emotion. There was the sun and the grass and the occasional scattered magazines, bagged dog shit, and flyers, and then there was Agatha. A pigeon started cooing in its nest.

'Basil,' said Jack, trying to concentrate, looking her in the eyes, breathing through his nose painfully; his own allergies were being triggered this season. 'Basil Alawi is in love with you.'

To say that what Agatha Darger did next was spit and laugh at the ground is hardly fair to her, although it captures most of her response. She was reaching down inside herself and spluttering, coughing. Jack was standing over a barely sentient body that simply digested, heard, and consumed what it heard. She was not herself. She loitered. She kicked a stone. She was almost sick. Nothing happened.

Jack didn't want to ask if she were all right in case he misinterpreted whatever developments she was undergoing and made everything worse for her.

'And ...' she said.

'And?' said Jack. 'What do you mean *and*? I'm trying my best here, Agatha!'

'And ...' she said, quietly, and broke into her first real sob. '*Mr Hussein.*'

Still, nothing happened. Jack stared into space, and a fat, black shape seemed to clog out the sun. But nothing happened. A chasm seemed to open directly under his feet, and nothing happened.

'Mr Hussein?' said Jack.

Agatha nodded, spluttering and he saw the red stain on her sleeve and wondered where it had come from and thought of his childhood and thought of the surgeries that Fauna had spoken about, and he heard the Arab on the war memorial's voice ringing in his ears about *white* pussy', and he stared into space, and although nothing happened he could not for three seconds close his own mouth. In St Michael's, in his memory again, Jack saw the fat, obsidian shit-eating grin of Mr Hussein looking over not only himself but, clearly, Agatha through the crack in the church doorway; Basil, his accomplice, merely quivering behind him, amazed at what the man was capable of. Jack remembered English class. He wiped sweat from his face, and when he removed his hands again, he saw Agatha's bloodshot eyes that pulsed tears so heavily he thought that they would pop. And this was real life.

'You get it now ... *fucking*,' she said, lightly. 'Do you, Jack?'

'I get it,' he said. 'I get it. I get it. I get it.'

Agatha pulled up her blouse and showed a wound around her belly that he barely got the sense of and yet absolutely did not want to see again. He got it; he didn't get it; he got it.

'Do you know what my—my *dad* would have done? He'd have killed him,' Agatha said. 'He'd kill him if he were alive. He would *kill* them.'

Agatha didn't want to be hugged, let alone touched. Yet when she wanted to, when her eyes looked for a moment to plead with him, Jack knelt down and let her dig her scabrous, nervously chiselled-down nails into his cheeks, pull them, dig into his arms and hands. It was clear she hated everything that came within her grasp.

'Do you want me to kill them?' he thought. 'Should I *kill them?*' he whispered to Agatha.

She threw her arms up as though about to have a seizure, spluttered, and listened to the sound of the pigeon coo.

'*I don't know!*' said Agatha. Now came the hyperventilation. 'I told my mum, and I told Mr Thompson, and I told Frederick Williams, and I told Basil Alawi, and I told Jamal Yusuf, and he *fucking* laughed at me! And now I have told Jack Grundon who is not a Muslim, who is English, who is fucking autistic or something, and I don't know what's going to happen!'

Jack hugged her, and she hit him again, sprawling, and he let her go once more, knowing now that whatever affection he could foist on her physically was diseased, was misplaced, must be prevented, aborted, and that *they* must be stopped.

Agatha stood on her own and cried. She cried and cried, and she didn't want tissues. Jack just stood there and breathed, and Agatha cried for her father, a former policeman, and she did not want to be comforted. It was dismal. She described, breathing in bursts, how he had a great record of arresting dangerous men and how he used to get into bar fights and was a great security guard in his youth, and then, and then she told him, he was murdered. He had no gun or anything—didn't like having them. He was arresting an Albanian for drug possession. The guy had a shank in his pocket, in London, and he had just stabbed him, straight into the heart, stabbed him, and that was it. And now she had been raped repeatedly, and he was dead—and Basil had said he wanted to 'marry her', even rescue her from the clutches of Mr Hussein, Agatha said, and nobody cared.

'Because nobody *ev*-er cares ...' panted Agatha, '—not even when you talk about it!!'

Jack could not calm her, did not want to, and knew not what to do. He was feeling a new emotion. What might it be called? He saw Agatha and gazed at the pathetic cuts she had made in his arms and then at the moon in the far distance of the sky.

'You're a boy. You're a man. You hate this!'

Jack quivered.

'I *know* you hate it. You cried like a fucking bitch during that poem! I saw you. You did, Jack. You hate what's happened? Don't you hate what's happened to me?—*Shut up!*'

Jack said nothing. No line in particular, simply the title of the poem came back to him: *Colonisation in Reverse*. He realised that his stupidly embarrassing but nonetheless honest tears had marked him out, had made it plausible to Agatha that he would understand her. He caught himself almost smiling at the divine strangeness of life.

'Don't go to the police with this,' Agatha said. 'They're friends with them. With *them*. They're *THEM*!'

Jack remembered the Pakistani head of local police. He drew constellations, networks, in that moment, he had never had the strength to draw before. He saw an alliance of students, of teachers, of *a people*, a people who felt no qualms about humiliating their enemy, about doing absolutely anything. He gathered himself, and he left the realm of the political, and maybe he circulated Jupiter and Mars for a time. And then he came back to Earth. And then there was Agatha Darger, this girl, the Pakistanis, the group, the gangs undoubtedly, and Basil Alawi, the Alawite, and rape. When did she start bleeding from wherever the stains of blood were coming from?

He remembered his own age and cursed whoever had planned, enabled, or culturally organised the 'phenomenon' he was experiencing. That would be a lot of people. As Agatha talked and cried and sometimes silently screamed, Jack knew that he had reached the culmination of his youth. Not only could he not go back to being a child again after this, or be so irresponsible as to suppose that even doing that would be at all moral, but he was willing, for the first time, to acknowledge that all his childhood had been a lie, a lie that enabled *this*. This was because the idealistic aspects of his youth had barely alluded to the reality that was before him in his own town, his own class, in Agatha. It was also because everything that had not been some joyful distraction enabled by his mother, most of the time—reading Shakespeare, for instance—had been little more than an attempt to psychologically destroy him enough so that he, Jack, would refuse to go out and *kill* those who had raped Agatha now. For him, rather, the molestation had been psychological. He had been subjected to the mulching of manhood such that the English women, the little girls, would have no defense from the likes of him. It was deliberate. It must have been deliberate, all along, whether it was some teacher like Miss Wright or the archetype of Miss Wright who was originally responsible or whoever paid the piper, funded her, her type in government, in media, in schools. The chimera smiled.

(He thought. He could not look at Agatha. He thought.)

But it must not have worked, Jack told himself, or at least, not all of it yet. Because Jack was filled with rage, just rage now. Whatever the lying news said the next day about how this had never happened or it was overestimated or it wasn't *all* the Muslims in the school or even most of them who were complicit in the rape, the rapes (he hadn't even asked about the others), or, eventually, how it had never happened whatsoever, and it was the 'Far Right', angry vengeful husbands and fathers and sons, who were really evil, Jack didn't care. He told himself he couldn't care. He told himself that this was the end.

He knew what he had witnessed all his life. And here was the culmination of his life. Was it some grand adventure in another land? Was it some invention, or an inspiring career as a scientist or writer? No, it was not. It was a raped girl in a field losing her mind because she knew that what had happened to her didn't count, or was justified, because the one who had perpetrated it was a Pakistani, and she had white skin, and that, in the minds of the principalities, the powers, whoever they happened to be, was enough to make it all make sense. The culture willed what had happened and wouldn't apologise, and she screamed with the pain of feeling this and everything else.

What more was there to be said? Jack couldn't say anything to Agatha's whimpering. He did not even want to connect all the dots that brought her here to this moment before him. He would prefer never to have been told. Now, an investigation occurred everywhere in his head. What was it that they were living under? It was not a democracy. It was not something that any of their grandfathers had fought for in the war. What *was* it they were living under? He could not find the word. He tried to, to distract himself from Agatha. He would do anything to distract himself from Agatha. He could already see the coming late nights, the hours of TV, of hearing alternate narratives than the one he had just heard. Yet that, yet all those—all were lies, would be lies, must be lies. The gravity of the situation before him was irrefutable. What had happened to Agatha had happened and would continue to occur until he did something about it. But what could he, a boy, in all seriousness do?

He could stand here with Agatha, wait for her to finish weeping, and just be present with her, hold the secret she had unveiled in his heart. He could tell his mother, who was terrified of Arabs. He could confront Mr Hussein, whose lessons— even the one that day!—he would have to continue attending. He could, as he had already considered, contact the police.

'Aa.'—Agatha.

He could disbelieve what he had heard from Agatha, which, as he breathed in and out and half-closed and half-opened his eyes, seemed the easiest option. He didn't want to look at her and know what particular wounds and acts had been performed on her, this doll. He recognised, whenever he managed to hold his gaze on her, that she had been turned into an object for the relief of foreign men, a receptacle. She was his age. She was a young girl. Then she was a toilet. Then she was a girl again. And now, perhaps, she was the bride-to-be, at fifteen, of her English teacher from Kabul. He wanted, by Jesus Lord, to stop thinking and stop looking at her. But he could not help but think. He could not stop looking.

'Aa—*aa.*'

What happened next was that Agatha cried and cried for fifteen minutes, and Jack just stood and stared, feeling totally useless, that he had failed already to be strong enough, that all men had failed, all Englishmen, for this to be possible. He was further wrenched down from memories of the distortions of culture in the classroom and in the theatres and in the textbooks that he had formerly hated to realise that all these were meant to be the gifts of diversity to compensate for this, for the rape, for the rape at the centre of Bothelford, of England. These things might have been evil to the life that he had lived but not in comparison with the life that he lived now. When Agatha ran out of tears and then of lacrimal fluid to cry out, she stood there slightly in front of the green bars as the pigeon cooed, and she twitched. She tutted slightly and twitched. She looked like a video-game character that had gotten partly stuck inside a wall. She tutted. She twitched. She twitched. She stood there. She twitched.

It felt almost perverse for Jack to realise that now both he and Agatha were late for school. But what was school anyway anymore? Agatha was twitching. School did not exist. Agatha was twitching. The pigeon cooed in the tree.

'Do you want water?' said Jack, the skin around his own eyes, he assumed, beginning to peel off, and his forehead hurting like someone had stapled it with a stapler and then, he supposed, stapled it again.

'Ah,' she breathed. She removed her timetable from the inside of her blazer. It was laminated and small. Some lessons were crossed out with a red pen. She saw that today had no red pen on it and was somewhat relieved. She put the timetable away. She gathered her things and, craning her neck at a diminished height, covered her face. She walked. Jack stood as he was.

By accident, because the zip on her bag was broken and it had dropped out, she had left an orange Sainsbury's bag behind her on the ground with something inside it. Jack didn't want to look. Then Agatha came back and gripped the back of the Sainsbury's bag, screamingly, and whatever it was tipped out into the grass of the field, and neither did she look.

Agatha walked to school, registered at reception, and went to class. Jack felt his eyes burn and left the field without looking back. He didn't know if he was going to school. He decided, first, he was going to go on a walk through Bothelford, think, and hopefully, in that thinking, come to the end of thought. All of it.

'What can thinking even do for me?' Jack said, with a voice of entirely false irony. He felt like a substance was coming down from the top of his forehead and spreading down his abdomen and remembered the scene in the film *After Earth*, for some reason, where Will Smith's son finds a huge parasite embedding itself in his back. He walked through Bothelford. He observed the steadily accumulating rubbish, the tarmac, and he passed a kebab van with seals on its doors.

Later that day, a grandmother who lived opposite the field was doing her daily litter-pick, hunched with her stick to get all the randomly scattered leftovers of magazines and pizza boxes across the field into her bag for recycling. She went from one end to another as best she could, remembering all the while how nice the field had been during her childhood. Then, when she came to the end of the field and found a Sainsbury's bag in which clearly some steak had been and tidied that up, she saw before her an object that she had to put her glasses on to identify. Yet when she saw what it was, she didn't know whether to be upset for whoever had lost it or even a little angry that they should have been so careless as to abandon it. For it was a great waste to drop a brand new bicycle pump out on the field like that, as well as being destructive to the environment.

SIX

Instead of going to school, Jack continued to walk through Bothelford. He decided to *really* dwell on what his town was. He wanted to know what Bothelford had done to bring inside itself what he had just heard come out of Agatha. He wondered how he could have been fooled for so long that this was a safe place, that this was somewhere tribal warfare no longer occurred, whereas actually, Jack thought, it was a battlefield. And it had long been a battlefield before he was born. But now, instead of the battles occurring in a few courtrooms connected by phone line to the mayor's office or among non-government charity organisations dedicated to potentially rehousing foreigners, now they were superabundant, these battles; they were increasingly unavoidable and yet managed somehow to always take place just out of the public eye. There was war in the lives of thousands and thousands of children. Playground dynamics verged, increasingly, on war. War was inside the police. The TV didn't care. The chimera smiled. He walked.

Out of the field and past the heaped rubbish was a nice walkway, partly cement and partly wood, depending on the age of the ground. The cement had come in during the nineties. There were bits of stone also beneath his feet every so often as he walked. He saw playgrounds of tarmac and three pubs in the distance away from the dim cloud-like exteriors of the school. He thought, 'Why not go? Why not have a peek at another region, or at least the worst of this one?' He thought about the film *The 400 Blows*, with the French kid running away from the borstal at the end and going and exploring just what it was that lay in front of him before reaching the sea, the end of the movie, and having nowhere else to go, stopping. The film flickered out of his head; why was Jack thinking about films? Time to change the topic. After all, Jack had his grades. His grades were sorted! His grades were allotted, even, in lines of Cipralex tablets. Today, he could afford a mental breakdown. 'Why not?' And was he, Jack, going to kill them?

He couldn't, but if he could, would he? In the street past his school, he heard the bell that began the first period after registration. Above him in the blue sky with slashes of grey clouds, a plane hung like a floating coffin. The leaves of an oak tree flecked by him as he stared up at it. Not quite opposite the school, but a little along from it, was an old manor house made of the same red brick as the school chapel. Birch trees were planted in front of it, though they didn't offer whoever lived there much shelter from the gaze of passing crowds. As for the windows, they were broad like staring, astonished eyes. They had a view of the field, its accumulating rubbish from their height. The curtains in the windows were appropriately tattered and lowered. When you thought about the windows like eyes, these curtains looked like heavy eyelids, sagging and desperately trying to close themselves over the astonished eyes so that the whole structure could at last fall asleep, die with dignity. But Jack knew the house couldn't die with dignity. It was part of Bothelford.

Farther along the road was a bit of graffiti, although it was stylised enough that Jack could wonder if it were permitted to remain there by the parish council due to its quality, or even if it had been established by their sponsorship of a young up-and-coming 'Street Artist'. The graffiti defaced a red brick wall partly connected to the old manor house, and it depicted a boy holding a bright red box but wearing a blue and black school uniform and a cap. The boy's face was shadowed as in a gritty detective comic or a piece of military propaganda. He had white circles for eyes, no pupils. Jack never knew when he passed it whether it was intended to criticise as soulless the lower-middle-class people who historically attended his school, like himself, or whether it was intended as a strange, secret compliment. It looked like him. It looked vengeful. He walked on.

Jack hadn't expected the filling up of the schools of Bothelford to so empty its streets during the day. Occasionally, there were men smoking outside a Turkish barbers, but few others remained in the street. Some loitered, some went on their way. Jack came to a crossroads by a defunct model shop made of ugly brown brick. He decided he would go left and keep going left.

Two buildings along, he had once seen an Englishman get into an embarrassing fight with a Sikh running an off-licence store. How old had he been, six? The Englishman back then was obviously on drugs (presumably not Cipralex) and punched the knot or turban or whatever it was right off the Sikh's head. The hair had scattered like cobwebs. Little Jack had cautiously watched. Then a fat woman, wearing a pink dress, started yelling from three stories up in a surprisingly old building across the road. In front of Jack, there had been a blonde woman, well-dressed, in a long raincoat, and she had been screaming. She had been screaming for the police about the incident. Little Jack had been slightly horrified. Then he had walked down, not to St Michael's, but to another church, wondering if he were going to get whatever equivalent of a turban he had himself busted off his own head by the same crazy Englishman. He had escaped past the model shop only to find himself nowhere more comforting than a graveyard.

Now, Jack passed that same area and recalled, in his early youth, what had happened there. He must have been seven, at least. The decaying, leaning graves were still there, and obviously, probably hundreds and hundreds of skeletons underneath. There had, in fact, been stories in his father's generation about there being so many bones in that dense space that, by force of will, Jack supposed, they had pushed themselves up. Shinbones still came up every so often.

Anyway, six- or seven-year-old Jack Grundon had gone into the graveyard in order to get away from the violent Englishman. There, he had seen an old man with a white beard with brown stains in it. The man was crouching, squatting like a gremlin with a dented head. *A sorcerer, a kind of male witch?* Little Jack had wondered this, had gone over to this man, and had decided to ask him what exactly he was doing. The man hadn't been poorly dressed. But he had, indeed, been digging the ground of a flowerbed parallel to the graves. Jack had asked. The man had turned, and little Jack had seen that the homeless and demented man before him was eating the soil, that he was putting handfuls of the soil of the flowerbed into his mouth, that it was dry, that it looked like brown faeces or just sand. Then the man had stuck his tongue out at little Jack, and little Jack had seen his black oesophagus, or he imagined that he saw it. Some imprecise wall or bundle of soot and guts was what he saw. Like the interior of a ghost.

Today, Mad Jack (now he would think of himself as mad occasionally) scanned the graveyard, and there was obviously no homeless man there anymore. There were bundles and piles, even mounds of cigarette butts sticking out of a nearby bin that hadn't been cleaned. Jack saw a rat that was bigger than his left calf muscle skitter by over a shattered bottle of Hobgoblin. So he had died. The stranger had shown his condition to Jack as if to initiate him into a life of gradually dying, and then he had rotted away into nothing. That was appropriate enough. And that man had actually been some mother's infant at a certain time. He wondered whether, looking into the tar-coloured eyes of her newborn many years ago, his mother had had some premonition that her baby would be eating soot and bird shit in the back of a shutdown church one day, and whether, on top of that, she had ever prayed at the same church when she was alive. Mad Jack passed the church now, hair sprawling in all directions or feeling as if his hair could do only that.

They had kept the sign saying 'All Saints' above the door, and Mad Jack considered the possibility that when he had encountered the madman, having been separated from his father that day on a school run, the crazy old freak had originally gone to the graveyard to commune with his own boyhood. Was it possible that the man had gone there and started putting dirt in his mouth and over his grotty beard in order to resurrect some childhood memory? It was a nice idea.

Mad Jack reflected on this as he stepped past the sandy, brutalist front of the church's extension and saw two fat women who looked like disfigured pigeons having green tea with one another. The concrete vein of Bothelford that Mad Jack currently followed led into a number of sub-roads. One of these, to his right, was largely constructed out of brick, although not ancient by any means. This brick road, with red and even yellow brick, had been built during the late eighties by a functioning parish council. Plenty of cigarette butts were shoved in between the stones, mashed. Some bricks were broken in half. Some bollards were ready to tip over, having previously got mangled up by cars bumping into their sides.

That was one sub-road. But there was another road that was literally just oozed tarmac. It was lumpy, uneven, and new. This path on the left, hurting his feet as he trod on it, had the same abortive texture as everything else that was currently alive in England. He had a vision temporarily of all the woodland creatures—the sparrows, the red squirrels, the grey squirrels, the dead badgers he often saw by the side of the road, the pheasants, the red kites, the muntjacs and deer, hares, pikes, some lambs, some girl's horses, sleeping together—all crushed sorely and buried under that tarmac. He smelt lingering marijuana, hated the stink. It was the kind of smell that people brought to places when they despaired. That was silly too. Mad Jack remembered Agatha had been raped.

Jack looked past the pavement and into his hands and then through and up the veins in his hands, and he imagined something pouring inside them, long copper wire tendrils pumping it in, and his blood shooting out of his veins like Ribena, delicious, and then he looked back to the pavement. He looked at his slightly tattered shoes. He recalled he had left his sports bag and all but his laptop bag back in the field and cursed himself. That was a good £350's worth of stuff, or so his mother would say when he got back. His father would probably hit him if he found out.

Possibly the bags weren't gone yet, and someone hadn't stolen them. But Jack knew he wasn't going back to collect them and that he had shed them. He bit the end of his left index finger near the top, and it bled a little. He stopped. He decided he was going to follow this path on the left all the way down, wherever it went and however it continued. He continuously struck the ongoing bleeding bite wound against his blazer, drew a St George's Cross by mistake on his white shirt. He effaced it. He wiped a little bit of the blood around his mouth, checked his reflection, and removed all the marks with spit as best he could. For some reason, he wondered whether English adults were frightened of injured children just as Muslim women seemed to be terrified of dogs. Maybe this wasn't a good idea, and by coating himself with blood, as well as having white skin, he was signalling that it was all right for him to be attacked or something. What even had been the idea behind it all? Mad Jack thought of Agatha. He stared at the pavement.

Once upon a time, Bothelford had dreamed of a fairy-tale princess from Denmark, and now Somalis exchanged crack cocaine at the back of a halal chicken shop at the end of the street where she used to dance and sing her arias. How many children of this ancient mother of Bothelford were still left? The advertising around portrayed black and Muslim men and never her descendants alone, and if they were permitted to show up at all then they *must* be subordinate to the foreigners—especially the white women must be. This went for advertising at the gambling dens, the tourist agencies, educational institutions, internships for banks and news agencies, anything the TV could get its claws into. Adverts, thought Jack, came from a demographic future where there were only a few white people left in Britain, and the red-haired and blonde women with blue eyes were all married to sneering, but whitely effete husbands, darker than the black hole at the heart of the universe. The message of every advert seemed to be, 'You are going extinct, whites. Please go extinct. Have a lovely evening.'

Jack bit the ends of, not his fingernails, but the skin of his second and third fingers on his left hand. It wasn't like he was drawing blood this time, merely widening the loose tangle of skin under the nails a little bit. He was now extremely conscious that he had a heartbeat and various complicated organs inside of him. It was odd, and it was not odd at the same time. He wondered what it would be like to be pinned up against the wall by Mr Hussein or to cry madly in front of himself as a girl in a field. No, he didn't.

With the children gone for the day, Jack observed, Bothelford was a population of Romanians drinking Hennessy on a street corner, a homeless man playing a banjo while his ponytail curled like a blonde snake under his beret, a group of fifteen youths who could have been from any part of Africa or the Middle East or anything in between trying to rob JD Sports, as well as around a hundred intimidated, shuffling old white natives who outnumbered everyone else. The positions of the spines of these people implied chronic injury or a flat-out strain against what was in front of them. Had their spines twisted more, day after day, as the world in front of them grew easier to revile? Jack's spine felt mildly distended at the bottom, at least today. He went around with his hips slightly bent and an emotion so strong inside him it wouldn't cause him to get into a fight, and it wouldn't cause him to start crying. It was so strong that it felt like a bright, hormonal smoke of no particular colour had been released over his exposed brain tissue. It whimperingly touched him with its paws. He knew that weekend, when he got to his father's flat, the bare interior, that he was going to see if he could get the man to pour him as much red wine as possible, having seen first-hand the effect that sort of liquor had on his father's memory. Then came the underpass.

He imagined a martini-shaped light that glowed blue at the bottom of the basement of a bar. He imagined himself drinking at a future age, maybe twenty-five. Jack felt that his physical and mental age no longer overlapped. There was the sound of a coat hanger being used to remove a sticker of an abstract symbol from one of the underpass walls. As Jack passed under, the sky turned greyer, and he saw that there were two homeless tents filled up with some amorphous substance. One was green and had black netting and was quite expensive. The other one was small and red, and there was an organised collection of four different needles lined up from longest to shortest directly outside its opening. On the right side of the underpass, there was an Arab kneeling with a cardboard sign and a white cup that Jack recognised from the local Five Guys restaurant. His nose really did have a hook shape. A piece of paper that turned out to be the back of an old Penguin book on Egyptology was blowing amongst a pile of black leaves. A tent cackled. Jack exited the underpass slowly without looking the Arab, who appeared to be sleepy, in the eyes. He appeared to have vitiligo and black soupy pupils as an extension of that. Jack went up the pavement, passing a pregnant mother with mascara smeared on her chin and a young girl about two years older than him, and he couldn't tell if she was the woman's daughter. She was not.

Coming out of the underpass, Jack tried to read the inscription that had been carved by its exit; this was from the seventies, back when Bothelford had only one Imam, let alone five. Part of it was sprayed over with silver paint, but what remained read: 'From silent [ ] a multi-tongued town has grown.' Jack liked to imagine that the missing noun was 'Bothelford'.

From silent Bothelford, a multi-tongued town *had* grown; it was true. Jack pondered whether there was another thing, a silenced act that could fit in that space. And then Jack decided to ponder nothing at all.

Jack saw cigarettes, and he wanted to put a cigarette in his mouth and have it blacken his lungs like the anti-smoking teaching seminars had told him, and he wanted to breathe out gas and be gassed and feel nothing at all. Jack looked at the sky. There was an enormous, unoccupied tower in this part of Bothelford with nothing in it; it couldn't be demolished because nobody had gotten permission yet. It overshadowed a pub that was attached to its bottom floor, called The Goat, with an anchor for some reason strapped to its front. It was a house of the dead. The pub had black windows, and it looked like the kind of place that would be occupied by men who had just miserably retired and had tried but couldn't go through with actually killing themselves because in Great Britain the government doesn't allow you to buy a gun. Instead, Jack guessed, such men probably just thought about getting stabbed all the time by foreigners to make up for it. Indeed, Jack thought he had discovered from various facial expressions that day that the norm in Bothelford was that the men fantasised constantly about getting stabbed and having their stab wounds do the hard work that they were unwilling to inflict on themselves. *Fantasise* wasn't the right word. And what did the women think about?

Jack came to a bollard, past which a man who was fat right at the front of his stomach, to the extent that he looked pregnant, passed with a suitcase filled with tissues, dollars, and paper forms. Weirdly, he remembered his father's telling him about a since-gentrified area of London where 'an audience'—he didn't know to what, *to life itself?*—had sat, and smoked, and injected themselves with heroin every so often. Mad Jack wondered whether injecting the front of his brain with a needle full of heroin would delete his memory of Agatha. Perhaps!

He opened the door of the bar and felt like people's gazes were crowding into him like dirty pieces of cardboard. That was the correct metaphor. The barman was clearly one of those who was willing to serve a young man, if not a child, if not an infant, but wouldn't sell you orange juice of any kind. He looked like a kind of pale, wolf-human hybrid that had been mad at a certain point but now was just so drained of energy that rage was meaningless for him to express.

'Water,' said Jack.

There wasan Ulster-Scotsman playing snooker with himself, and seemingly against himself, going around one side of the table and saying, 'That was a shot, eh, weren't it like?' before going around the other side and saying, 'Nae, it wasn't a shot!', and with so few variations it came across like a kind of extremely well-prepared but absolutely unimpressive stand-up act. The couches were red and had dents in them. Men who might as well have had no faces sat on them. All the teeth on the far left and far right side of Jack Grundon's mouth suddenly hurt. The man behind the bar shut his eyes and noiselessly poured the boy a glass of water underneath the giant brown tower that looked like it wanted to collapse on all of them. (*You couldn't see the building directly, and yet you felt its presence. If it were derelict enough, you could always die under it along with everyone else.*)

Mad Jack drank. He was drinking in a pub, even if it was water. He looked at the red star and the mark left by a hammer-and-sickle on the side of the left wall; he worked out that this had once probably been a Soviet bar before receiving certain complaints. He went back to drinking his water. He felt like a seven-year-old sucking a lollipop in such a way as to pretend he's got a cigarette in his mouth. Jack pulled out his phone and started absent-mindedly browsing on it. He wondered what he was going to look up. He went and sat in the corner by a destroyed wooden doll that might have been meant to be General Zhukov but could scarcely be qualified as a decoration now. But Jack's search was automatic. He didn't like to think about the crazy, drunk man in the back coming over and looking at his phone, so he kept it to himself. He hunched over.

The article that came up was by someone called Ella Hill; this was a pseudonym used by a victim from Rotherham who was writing for *The Independent* about her experiences; it was from 2018; Jack would have been around eleven years old when it came out. Jack decided to read a random paragraph midway through the article. One paragraph quickly became three. He drank water in between each paragraph. Occasionally, he looked behind him to check if the barman was seeing what he was looking at. He felt dirty. These were the paragraphs:

Religious indoctrination is a big part of the process of getting young men involved in grooming gang crime. Religious ideas about purity, virginity, modesty and obedience are taken to the extreme until horrific abuse becomes the norm. It was taught to me as a concept of 'othering'.

'Muslim girls are good and pure because they dress modestly, covering down to their ankles and wrists, and covering their crotch area. They stay virgins until marriage. They are our girls.'

'White girls and non-Muslim girls are bad because you dress like slags. You show the curves of your bodies (showing the gap between your thighs means you're asking for it) and therefore you're immoral. White girls sleep with hundreds of men. You are the other *girls. You are worthless and you deserve to be gang-raped.'*

Jack left the article. He found another one that mentioned the name Charlene Downes. Jack looked up Charlene Downes and saw that there were rumours that her body, after she had been raped and murdered, had been ground up into kebab meat. She had been fourteen; Jack wondered if her killers had found it funny to feed kebabs made out of her to drunk Englishmen and women. It was completely insane. This was the world of Count Dracula and Hollywood serial killers. It was more than that. It was the world of violence so depraved it became comic, something out of Punch and Judy or a *Looney Tunes* cartoon. It wasn't real, or not merely real. Jack twitched.

He slid his white headphones over his head. He got an odd look from the barman, although the barman didn't care. Jack played ambience to calm himself. He found a PDF. It was a document titled 'Independent Inquiry into Child Sexual Exploitation in Rotherham'. It was written by an investigative journalist named Alexis Jay, and it was from 2013. Jack would have been six years old when it was published. Again, he went to a random section:

> *They told us that children would be reluctant to seek help because they would be ashamed and also afraid that they would be placed out of the area far away from their families and friends. One young person told us that 'gang rape' was a usual part of growing up in the area of Rotherham in which she lived.*

He skipped.

> *Child B (2001) was referred to Risky Business by her school when she was 15 years old. By that time, she had been groomed by an older man involved in the exploitation of other children. Child B loved this man and believed he loved her. He trafficked her to Leeds, Bradford and Sheffield and offered to provide her with a flat in one of those cities. A child protection*

referral was made but the social care case file recorded no response to this. The case was discussed at regular Key Players meetings (no records of these meetings have survived). Within just a few months, Child B and her family were living in fear of their lives. The windows in their house were put in. She and her family received threats that she would be forced into prostitution. Child B was assaulted by other victims at the instigation of the perpetrator. An attack on her older sibling by associates of the perpetrator resulted in him being hospitalised with serious injuries. Child B also required hospital treatment for injuries she sustained. A younger child in the family was threatened and had to go into hiding so that the perpetrators could not carry out threats against her. Child B and her mother refused to have anything more to do with the Police, because they believed the Police could do nothing to protect them. Child B had been stalked and had petrol poured over her and was threatened with being set alight. She took overdoses.

He skipped.

Child N (2013) was 12 when extremely indecent images of her were discovered on the phones of fellow students. There were suspicions that older men and one woman had groomed her via Facebook.

Jack stopped and asked the crazy Ulster-Scotsman at the back of the bar to buy him a shot of vodka, which he kindly did. The barman wasn't interested enough in him to prevent him from drinking it. Jack swallowed the vodka, and it stung badly as it flowed down his throat. His head immediately started pulsing. Jack removed two Cipralex tablets from inside their container, and he was asked to leave the bar immediately, because they were not going to have him disrespecting the premises by taking his drugs out in the open like that.

'You could have at least used the toilet!' the barman shouted.

When Jack went out on the street, he walked, or ambled (which is a better way of putting it), down the lane on his left and saw one of Bothelford's largest mosques with two empty glass office buildings by either side of it. All three looked empty. One of the posters outside the mosque, which, again, he would later see in London on the tube, read: 'In paradise, gardens, vineyards, full-breasted *maidens, a full cup of wine. (Quran 78:31-34), Learn more at: DiscoverTheQuan.co.uk*'. And there was a barcode underneath which he could scan, if he liked.

Jack walked past the mosque and went to a newsagent's and bought a bottle of water for £3.70 and couldn't work out if the Arab proprietor was deliberately charging him more for being white. He hadn't looked him in the eyes when he bought it. Then he went outside on the street and drank the water. He placed three Cipralex tablets in his mouth and drank it all. He went back in the shop and asked to buy another water for £3.50 this time, and he was allowed to pay that much. Jack left.

He walked further along the street and realised he was coming around to where the war memorial was, which was dedicated to the brave sacrifices of two generations of men, including his own great-grandfather, but who, obviously, looking around at Bothelford today, had really died for no purpose at all.

Rather than the drunk Arab man sitting on top of it, this time it was a pale Muslim woman wearing a pink headscarf, looking melancholically off into the distance. As Jack approached her, he recognised in her slight sneer the same delight in occupying the monument as the Arab had. Jack walked up to her, coughing and feeling that he was going to vomit up his first drink along with his breakfast that morning, and asked her, 'Hey, what are you doing there? It's a war memorial. What are you doing up there?'

She looked at him scornfully, turned her head, didn't answer.

In the far distance, there were the sounds of school bells. As Jack loitered, beginning his walk in their direction, he realised that they were the leaving bells, and that the day was over. On Friday, he remembered, he had a Maths test coming up, and he was meant to email Fauna about the homework for their additional Physics lessons, as well as enter an English essay competition. He also needed to tell his mother about not wanting to do a language for A Levels, because she was pretty set on his learning German, and she had found that to be her favourite subject, personally, when she had taken it.

But then Jack laughed to himself and thought about Agatha. He thought about Mr Hussein. He thought about what he had read and what he had heard. He felt the vodka inside of him intermingle strangely with his Cipralex tablets, to the extent that he was experiencing a kind of temporary, world-spinning high. And Jack knew then that school absolutely didn't matter in comparison. There was no way he could take it seriously again.

SEVEN

When Jack returned home to his mother's house, the stench of vodka on him was more concerning to her than his absence from school, although that too had been reported. The short of it was that Jack told her that he had been having strange thoughts, that he had heard terrible things, and she was immediately concerned that he was having an adverse reaction to his Cipralex. She snatched the pill bottle out of his hands and read the side effects over and over again, checking them off one by one in comparison with whatever symptoms Jack seemed to express.

He was certainly drowsy. Mary asked if he was drowsy once, and then asked him if he still felt drowsy—('Yes.') She ran through the other options, asking if he had had diarrhoea ('No.'), mood swings ('Yes.'), migraines ('Yes.'), hallucinations ('No.'), depression ('Maybe.'), or chronic feelings of emptiness ('Always.'). Mary Phillips decided to call up Mia, the therapist, straight away—and, given it was still 4:30 p.m., hoped that she would be able to catch the woman before her office closed at 5. This failed to work because Mia's secretary told her that Mia was 'on her break' and was legally permitted to be on it for an extra half hour due to overworking a few minutes on the day before; this was in her contract. So Mary put the phone down, and asked Jack to go to bed, although he wasn't tired, before calling up Jack's father about the medication in order to talk with him about it and quiet her own trembling nerves. This caused an enormous argument when Jack's father arrived since Mary still hadn't told him about Jack's being on medication. Even during the call, the man was practically hissing down the end of the phone, horrified at what was happening to his son, at the same time as he enjoyed using this ammunition to snipe at his ex-wife.

From all this, Jack let himself fade away. None of it mattered. Jack's medical situation was clarified with the school, and he didn't get into trouble for missing a day. All he received were a few odd looks from his form tutor and a few questions, every so often, from the matron about whether he ever needed to talk about anything. He told her that if he could think of anything really important worth mentioning, whilst staring at the ceiling and visualising the exact, nightmarish acts that he would have to report if he were being serious, then he would bring it up.

The next time Jack saw Agatha she was collecting a box of red-ribboned chocolates from her pigeonhole in the school's post-office room. She walked with a crutch. She wore acne-concealer makeup over one half of her whole face as if to cover what was actually a region of her exposed skull. The floor was carpeted and blue. Jack was just there to register at the reception desk after receiving a check-up from the matron before school. They looked at each other immediately, and didn't say anything. Briefly, Jack looked elsewhere from this girl who had been deeply bruised. Inexplicably, a joke perhaps that one generation had told itself and another had forgotten, there was framed on the wall just above Agatha's head a photograph of a British soldier wearing a black coat. The soldier was leaning next to a Lewis gun, a massive firearm with a loading wheel that spun around its core. He held it like a shepherd would a staff.

'How are you?' said Jack.

'... I'm good. ...'

Time had started again. Time had not existed between when Agatha had confessed and now. But now it had started again. Jack realised he was in an extension of the same conversation they had had before, the confession in the field, and he stared into the ceiling. He looked into her void of a face. And it absorbed him. In all likelihood, Agatha was going to start crying again right there in front of him, or she was going to hit him as he felt he deserved for doing nothing to help. Nothing had changed.

Further than that, he was feeling all of it. Jack wasn't numb. The tablets he took that morning hadn't worked. As for the overdose of Cipralex he had taken the day before, whatever remained of its influence had clearly been cancelled out by the vodka, or at least its potency had been reduced by a sizeable enough amount that now the searing pain of responsibility and paralysis was all before him. Maybe yesterday's alcohol had dissolved today's medicine.

'What are you doing to help me?' said Agatha.

Jack felt as if he had, whilst sleepwalking, cut the throat of someone he loved, and now he was awake to what he or that other self had done.

'I ...'

Already, staring over the swollen veins in Agatha's forehead and the sort of clown makeup she had spread over herself to hide them, Jack could see the tears start to swell. For a moment, he sincerely fantasised about an alternate reality where he went to an American school and this had happened, and he could pretty easily, if he wanted to, go to a gun show with his father, buy a handgun—and here, and now, blissfully, shoot himself in the head. Why not dream of turning the gun on Basil Alawi or Mr Hussein? Due to the fact that, even in fantasy, he knew that such a reaction would erase the crime he sought to punish. The headline would be: 'WHITE extremist incel murders Muslim Scholar'. Jack lost himself in his head.

Agatha was still staring at Jack. Jack stood there and waited for the receptionist to finish signing him in. Agatha's look demanded something. Jack could do nothing. Jack wondered if the box of chocolates Agatha had received, given it was already months past Valentine's Day, was the gift of a family member. But Jack knew what it really was. It was an apology gift from Mr Hussein, or some relative of his, or Basil's, who had been additionally rough on some night that week. Hence the crutch, the makeup. Jack stared.

Agatha looked like a broken doll, but with bulging veins in her head. Did Jack need to listen to her at all? Could he simply go back to his life and ignore her?

Jack decided he was going to say something.

'*I am going to the police station*,' Jack said.

He said it calmly and clearly, although it pained him.

Agatha sighed: 'I went yesterday.'

'You ... good. Great. What do you think will happen?' said Jack.

Agatha shook her head at him, shifting it pathetically in the tiny socket of her neck joint.

'Are they going to investigate?' Jack said.

'I ... was *dropped*,' said Agatha.

'So your mum dropped you. What did you say?'

'No.'

'No?'

'No, she didn't drop me. I didn't say anything.'

Jack went quiet and thought. After a moment, he began to understand what had happened and clutched his brow.

'You get it?' said Agatha. '*They* dropped me.'

'They dared you to go and tell the police. ...' said Jack. 'They dropped you off at the police station afterwards and dared you to go in and report what had happened.'

'... *I got whips in my drive, pretty women in my bed* ...' Agatha recounted the lyrics of a song.

'What did you think they were going to do to you?' said Jack.

Agatha was staring into space. She pulled out her phone with the hand she had free from the crutch and opened a weblink that had been sent to her by a blocked number she couldn't contact back. Jack looked. There were two images.

The first of them was a painting, and the description from Wikipedia that was included underneath said that it was by the artist Otto Pliny, and it was called *The Slave Market*. The painting was set in the desert. It featured a pair of smiling Bedouins showing off two white sex slaves in front of their friends, who seemed interested in buying them. One of the women was wearing very light, semi-transparent robes. The other woman was exposed, completely naked but for a cloth in front of her vagina. Her expression was petrified, humiliated. She couldn't believe that this was happening to her. A smiling Bedouin held her by the shoulders.

'I can't tell if that's meant to be me or my Mum,' Agatha said.

She showed him the second image. It was a heavily pregnant, Somali bride with her clitoris removed. Someone had tirelessly photoshopped her with white skin. Jack stopped looking.

'They would do that to you. ...' He was originally thinking of asking this as a question, but immediately realised that they absolutely *would* do that to Agatha, having done so much to her already. He decided to ask something different. 'Does your mother know?'

'Yes and no,' said Agatha.

'Explain.'

'I don't want to talk about it.'

'I want to talk about it. How did this happen?'

'Jack Grundon,' said the receptionist. 'I have signed you in. Talk about whatever this is with Agatha in the main area. Don't loiter around here unless you're going to help her with her crutch.'

Jack turned back to the scornful fat woman in a trouser suit. 'Yes, Miss.'

Agatha's eyes had rapidly grown more bloodshot.

'Are you going to do something ...' Agatha said, 'or did I ask the wrong guy?'

'I'm going to do something,' said Jack. 'I just don't know what; I don't want to go to prison.'

He picked up one of her bags and the box of chocolates and opened the door for her. Agatha nodded and limped out into the main concrete area with him.

'Do you know Jessie Waters?'

'No,' said Jack.

'She's nine. She's not in big school yet. She's got black hair, and she wore a bandage on her eye once and said that it was because of surgery. Yesterday, Muhummad Akbar from your form group went up to her, and he threatened to rape her.'

Jack stared.

'Stop staring,' said Agatha. 'He said: *Man wants to rizz you up or you white bitch are going to slob on my dick.*'

'... Was he quoting a song?'

'Then, he said, as I stood by her—like, it would've been about fifteen metres away from here—he said to her, '*If you think I'm playing around, I want you. And I am going to hit you in the bitch ass face with a knuckle duster and I am going to rape the fuck out of you if you disrespect me.'*

Jack, if asked later, would be unable to describe the impression left on him by Agatha's repeating these words.

'Every day outside of school now, he waits with his big brother in this Lamborghini they've bought. And Jessie's mother has to run in and snatch her before they do. Every time. Her father works in London for a sewage company. He's not there.'

'Why don't you tell the school?'

Agatha almost laughed. 'The school know about it and have told Jessie and me to sit tight because they are doing *something* about it.'

'What did the police say?'

'I didn't speak to the police because I don't want to be fucking cut in half.'

Jack breathed, and his tube of medicine jostled in his pocket.

'What pills do you have?' Agatha snapped.

'Cipralex.'

'Give me.'

Jack slowly got the container out of his blazer, and Agatha snatched it from him, pulled out four tablets, and swallowed them on the spot.

'Agatha! What if you overdose?'

She cleared her throat, limped onwards, said: 'Numb.'

'I'm not leaving you.'

Agatha kept limping on. Jack carried what he could. She stumbled and almost tripped over a stone. There was a black lump on one of her ankles.

'Everyone is always doing *something* to help, and that something turns out to be nothing each time, and then it's the next time, and I go, or I'm brought, or I'm dared to see the police, or I go, and I meet, like, a social worker called Mr Singh, or whatever, and maybe I do that and then, what's going to happen is there's always going to be *something* done soon.'

Jack couldn't tell if Agatha wanted to unload the weight of what had happened to her or was simply shooting whatever words she could out of her mouth to keep herself occupied. He couldn't understand her, and he didn't want to, if he were completely honest. Out of nowhere, he wondered if one day this would be the fate of his own daughter. He pictured her face, her dark dot eyes melting into bruises. That, too, was an excuse to distract himself from Agatha.

'There's a group chat,' Agatha said. 'Called *white tings*; I've seen it.' She didn't elaborate.

The bell for the first period rang when they reached Tower A, and Jack and Agatha were meant to go in their separate directions because Agatha had History and Jack had Maths.

'Those tablets you have are *good*,' slurred Agatha. 'It's pretty obvious that you're useless as fuck, so bring me more if you want to help us out. O-K?—*Jessie and me.*'

'OK,' said Jack.

Agatha grinned, flashed again the bashed-in gap in her gums, and turned and limped into an elevator meant to be used only by disabled or paraplegic students. It was sleek and sterile. It could have just as easily been a gas chamber. She stood in it. She pressed the button. She went up. Jack imagined her entering heaven at the top of the elevator and the Lord, for once, asking to be forgiven for what he had allowed to happen to her.

Jack hadn't known her before any of this, so he was unable to determine if her personality had always been this way. Yes, she was a victim of inhuman degradation. She was also, or had been made into, a pretty bad person. Having been used, Jack felt, she had grown used to seeing only how others were useful. He also felt she had every right to feel the way she did, and she would never be the same. He went to his Maths class and stared at the wall for the whole hour.

EIGHT

Jack did nothing for some months. He turned sixteen. Nor did anything seem to happen about Agatha. She returned to school some days more wounded than others. Bruises accumulated and vanished. He did nothing. He took his Cipralex. She took his Cipralex. He began to get seriously concerned that he would one day be prosecuted as her drug dealer. He nearly hit Fauna Williams in the face for grabbing his backside in the dark when Mr Miles left the room during their after-school Physics session. His parents wondered how he had become so numb, unfeeling, and drained. On some weekends, he would speak to no one and do nothing more than stroll around Bothelford collecting with his bare hands what rubbish bothered him. He couldn't tolerate the town becoming any worse than it now was. Yet from Saturday to Sunday, he was often amazed to see just how much rubbish would accumulate and how quickly.

Beyond what can loosely be termed his 'professional' interactions with Agatha (where his roles were alternately medic, counsellor, and punching bag), Jack spoke with her more than anywhere else at that time on Telegram, if that can even be classified as speaking. Jack quickly noticed at the beginning of these communications that interfacing with Agatha—now that was the correct word!—was akin to talking to an amalgam of several very different people.

There was Agatha, the singer, who sent him pictures of herself as an eleven-year-old dressed, oddly enough, as Siouxsie Sioux, the goth musician. Often, she proudly blew a fake, folded paper cigarette. There was Agatha the slob; she sent him perhaps one hundred little clips of the sitcom *2 Broke Girls*, summarising her affection for Kat Dennings, the actress, and her character, Max. Jack thought of this personality as 'Agatha the slob' mainly because she unavoidably talked about the junk food she ate whilst binge-watching the series. Once she had apparently watched *2 Broke Girls* for six hours without her mother interfering, leading Jack to wonder under what circumstances this took place and what else was going on. There was also 'Dark Aggie', her elusive and dramatic alter ego. Agatha would put on makeup to summon her forth, usually blue around the eyes, before attaching long, extended, sleek black eyelashes. As she was expected to at other times, she would dress far beyond her age to complete this persona, photograph herself, and luxuriate in her own beauty. She would upload her 'dark pictures' to Instagram. They weren't for Jack, although occasionally she seemed to appreciate his input.

After sending him a photograph of her wearing a big witch's hat that Halloween with fake fangs in her mouth and blood pouring out of it, Agatha messaged Jack in a way that he found amusing. It was, in any case, better than when 'Dark Aggie' randomly decided to send him pictures of gore, pigeons with their heads sawn off, war photos, compilations of men—sometimes hilariously—being kicked in the testicles.

AgathaD914:	*What dyuo think?*
JGFraiser:	*Idk. Cute?*
AgathaD914:	*lol no. What u doin tonight?*
JGFraiser:	*...*
AgathaD914:	*[gif of a black man shaking his head.]*
JGFraiser:	*What am I supposed to say to you?*
AgathaD914:	*That I'm hot, bitch!*
JGFraiser:	*You know you're attractive already. Why does my onion matter?*
AgathaD914:	*Lol, autocorrect.*
JGFraiser:	*[the painting, Wanderer above the Sea of Fog, by Caspar David Friedrich, 1818.]*
AgathaD914:	*GaY! –Am out with Mommy. Bye!*

Where she was going that evening Jack didn't ask, and nor did he bother to question what she was doing. The little vampire was surely up to something that was at least moderately pleasing to her, and Jack was at his happiest merely to know that she could still enjoy herself. Sometimes it was nice. He thought about messaging Agatha at the end of a long, boring day once in a while, and he even looked forward to it. Perhaps, Jack thought, this was the freedom that came with interacting with someone at the far reaches of reality who had already had everything possibly bad happen to them and whose living existence was, despite it all, a kind of miracle. He looked up the etymology of the name 'Agatha' one day after his own (his own being obscure: John, jackknife, steeplejack, animal male, ordinary man), and found that it derived from *agathos*, meaning 'the good'. Many, apparently, were named after the Sicilian martyr, St Agatha—this was 'Martyr Aggie', Jack called her, whose breasts were removed by tongs on refusing to denounce the vow of virginity she had made. In the story, Martyr Aggie had been reported by Quintianus, the Roman prefect who claimed her as his wife but knew she was a Christian and that this secret could be wielded to make the Romans punish her if she refused to submit to him. When she did refuse, Quintianus told the Romans and the Romans intended to burn her at the stake for her beliefs. And yet an earthquake prevented it. A miracle of God had set her free, before St Peter healed her wounds, and her name was divinised and spread around the world for almost a millennium.

On learning this, Jack let himself wonder if his own Agatha's suffering was somehow determined by her name, whether that name was in reality a curse, and whether the veneration of Agatha, of the good, in that arduous Christian manner which the story evoked did not have something endemically wrong with it. Other times, he considered that the human figure in agony approximates the angelic, the more-than-human, in a way that pure joy cannot grasp. He never spoke with Agatha about any of this, of course, but considered it as she sent him pictures of Snoopy the dog, late at night, whilst, he did not know, covering her head with a sheet and searching, once in a while, for the brightest star in the sky, Sirius—or, actually, it was the North Star, Polaris, with which she sometimes got it confused, and wrote to him, 'I miss home', under a strange dark roof in the middle of Bothelford. Jack did not know but supposed that Agatha didn't sleep often. Nor did he understand that when she dreamed, she dreamed always of wings, of farms at the end of the world, and of her cat, Jenny, with a red bow she had bought and lost, that was presented to her again by God, her father, like a badge she had won at Brownies when she was nine.

Then it was 2024. An eighteen-year-old Rwandan stabbed thirteen English girls in a dance class, and three died. Muhammad Akbar and three others yelled out in the school assembly commemorating the event; one of the white girls in the school was a relative. There was a social-media account named after the killer discovered to be run by a girl named Disha, who idolised him in the same way that some American women idolised the serial killer Ted Bundy. Yet there was an undeniably anti-white element to Disha's affection, especially since she was neither Rwandan nor Muslim, but Indian. Jack didn't hear much more about this affair. But once when he passed by the girls' changing room to get to the boys', he heard the now almost familiar cry of '*White cunts ...*'.

On another day, the headmaster invited a representative from the non-government organisation Hope Not Hate to come to the school and discuss the dangers of white supremacy. But the event couldn't last, because the speaker's last name was Silverstein, and the Muslim students were at that time ever increasingly furious about Gaza. Jack wondered what knock-on effects Gaza would have on how Agatha was treated by her traffickers. Would they learn to see having sex with her as revenge for the ongoing conflict?

Meanwhile, Jack took his GCSEs; he got ten A stars. For A Levels, Jack chose English, Physics, and Mathematics. He chose English, not because he was good at it, but mainly because he wanted to keep an eye on Agatha, and Agatha wanted to do English. She both loved the subject, it seemed like, and—Jack supposed—couldn't keep herself away from Mr Hussein. For what consequences could follow her leaving his class? Or maybe it was love, and she loved him! Jack considered both possibilities. A very old concept he had recently stumbled across on Wikipedia was telegony, or the idea that a woman can become a vessel for the men she has had sex with and that, even against her will, she can infer their characteristics as a Ouija board is influenced by demons. Jack wondered whether love had been forced on Agatha at this microbiological, even spiritual level and whether this counted as decolonisation according to the academics who published books on the subject. Would they nod to Agatha as she begged at their expensive shoes? Or was love love, as they liked to say?

After hearing about his results down the phone, Jack's parents celebrated; they did not get back together or stop drinking. Next door, although no one noticed, Fatima had another baby, and her husband's new wife had two. They were silent as ever but for the occasional cry of a child.

Then, shortly after finishing his GCSEs, Jack started regularly returning to The Goat. After all, the barman had permitted him to drink underage and, when Jack went back there, he forgave him for taking Cipralex the last time. Now it was only ever Jack, the barman, and the crazy Ulster-Scotsman who went there, and the faceless guests had long faded away. The Goat was a business run either out of affection for the pub itself or it was a money-laundering scheme; Jack never asked the barman which it was. Whilst Jack's mind dulled into a set of rigid and true opinions, his liver burned and blackened adversely, or so he assumed. In the meantime, Jack generally stopped speaking with his parents about politics, then all things, knowing that if they couldn't understand what was happening at his school or refused to understand it for ideological reasons, then they couldn't be trusted to know about anything else in the real world. So Jack started a blog, started reporting on the things he had heard at the school, feared that any day he would get a knock on the door from the police, achieved no success in establishing an audience but continued nonetheless, hoping that one night, one might emerge.

In English, for A Levels, Jack had Mr Hussein and a new teacher called Miss Lawrence, who, in comparison to Mr Hussein's three legitimate sons, had no children of her own but was the same age and weight as her colleague. The two of them looked like alternate versions of each other. But whereas Mr Hussein smiled at and complimented Jack persistently, praise which he didn't even want, Miss Lawrence tyrannised Jack. She hated him immediately and would have preferred it if he had never joined her class, let alone bringing all his so-called opinions with him into it like a marauder. This was especially true because the text that they were studying for A Levels that year was a novel by a South African man named J.M. Coetzee, and it was called *Disgrace*. It was the story of a South African literature professor who, after having illicit sex or even raping one of his seemingly African students, was punished by the gods, or that's how it looked, in having his own daughter, Lucy, raped and impregnated by three African men. It was extremely well written. Agatha flinched in her chair when she heard it read sometimes.

Then, in one lesson, Mr Hussein impressed upon Agatha the duty of reading a very particular part of *Disgrace*, which she really didn't want to read but felt compelled both by his authority as her teacher and something more than that, that she had to.

When she read it, Jack temporarily felt alive in his shame again. Summer had passed with absolutely nothing of interest to Jack occurring in it. But here was time again. Here was the ongoing war. Here were his own pathetic delays. Here was Mr Hussein, the monster; here was Agatha hesitating and reading the most offensive part of the book. Here was Jack in his chair, as ever, doing nothing. Basil Alawi no longer went to English class. Agatha read, in her Estuary English voice, the words of raped Lucy and her father, David. First, it was Lucy who spoke out of Agatha.

'Nothing could be further from my thoughts. This has nothing to do with you, David. You want to know why I have not laid a particular charge with the police. I

will tell you, as long as you agree not to raise the sub-
ject again. The reason is that, as far as I am concerned,
what happened to me is a purely private matter. In
another time, in another place it might be held to be a
public matter. But in this place, at this time, it is not.
It is my business, mine alone.'

Then it was David.

'This place being what?'

Then one after the other, with Agatha deepening and raising her voice in tune.

'This place being South Africa.'
  'I don't agree. I don't agree with what you are doing.
Do you think that by meekly accepting what happened
to you, you can set yourself apart from farmers like
Ettinger? Do you think what happened here was an
exam: if you come through, you get a diploma and
safe conduct into the future, or a sign to paint on
the door-lintel that will make the plague pass you by?
That is not how vengeance works, Lucy. Vengeance is
like a fire. The more it devours, the hungrier it gets.'

It would be exaggerating to say that Mr Hussein was drool-
ing, yet the edges of his lips were pursed. Jack turned and
looked at him, and he couldn't deny that he saw a hungry joy

in them. After all, Mr Hussein was a fat man. He was the kind of man that even the black rapists in the novel would mock, laugh at, and jeer at. But he had done as they had, Jack knew, and more and worse to a young girl, to Agatha. And yet: what was the logic of the novel? What was the meaning of this section of it? Before he decided to do anything in response, Jack looked over the copy of the book in his hands and read over and over the lines '*This place being what?*' and '*This place being South Africa.*'

Jack wondered—now that Britain was being deliberately, actively turned into South Africa by those in government, by those who controlled what the TV broadcast, by those police officers who didn't investigate gang rapes for fear of being called racist—whether that was why Mr Hussein felt comfortable enough to boast like this. Jack tried to enfold himself in Mr Hussein's imagination and said to himself: 'I am going up, and you are going down, white girl. Down and up. This is vengeance, Agatha. Do you understand that I lived in Kabul and now I am here? Read the book, my Lucy, which you white people gave a Nobel Prize and put on school reading lists for men like me to teach. Did you think the plague would pass you by? No, Lucy. No, Agatha. *Vengeance is like a fire. The more it devours, the hungrier it gets.*'

All of a sudden, Jack was standing up, and Agatha, drained, had sat down. Jack was furious. He was filled with an abstract rage he didn't know what to do with. Was it again the white hormonal smoke that had toyed with his brain on the bad side of town? He felt like he was sweating it out from his forehead, even out of his eyes. 'Why did you make her read that?' said Mad Jack.

'What? Jack Grundon, don't int—'

'*Why did you make her read that, Mr Hussein?*'

Jack's was the kind of magnetic anger that demands a response, that tows a man in directions he wouldn't go by himself. Abdul Hussein forgot his authority.

'Because it's on the syllabus, Jack, and ...'

Mad Jack wanted to smirk but did not; the teacher was lost for words, looking around the classroom.

'... And,' said Mr Hussein, reconfiguring himself. 'It's a book about the Rainbow Generation, about multiculturalism, and the darker side of everything that men like Desmond Tutu and Nelson Mandela dreamed about. Do you know who they even are, Jack?'

'Yes.'

'Well, if you do, then you would also know that Britain is thankfully becoming a multicultural society also. That's why I'm here. That's why a third of the class are here, and since you've mentioned that you're partly Irish, it might even be why you're here.'

There were jeers at Mad Jack from a few of the students who were on their phones.

'Agatha is trying to talk to us about the difficult struggles of integration, and I mentioned at the beginning of the class, not that you were paying attention, that she did not have to read that section if she wanted. Thankfully, she is braver than you are.'

Mad Jack felt like sitting down but didn't. Miraculously, he didn't. His legs wavered, his left leg jittering slightly—a physical tick he hadn't managed to control. Jamal could tell from the back of the class that something was coming, and jokingly drew his thumb across his neck, and shook his head roughly, 'nah nah.' Mad Jack didn't even look at him when Jamal said something about a 'liddle slave owner', in a voice that was simultaneously as insulting as usual and more respectful than ever. Jack just breathed in.

'But, Mr Hussein, why that section?' said Mad Jack.

Mr Hussein seemed astonished that this usually considerate student was still talking.

'What section?'

'The section,' said Mad Jack. 'Where the female character justifies being gang raped by three African men who hate her for being a white woman in terms of historical vengeance, that you were grinning at, that the black students were laughing at, and that just Agatha was forced to read. Agatha is the only white girl here today.'

'Get out.'

'But sir—'

Mr Hussein slammed his hands down on the front of his desk. There seemed to be a sound delay. He opened his mouth. There was no noise. And then, all at once, the violence of what he said swept over Jack.

'Get ... OUT.'

Agatha whimpered from the other side of the room.

Mr Hussein was also sweating. He was sweating right through his thin, white shirt with grey lines decorating it like the bars of a cage. His hair was a wisp. His deep eyes looked the colour of tar. Jack realised this was not a teacher's anger at a student. This was tribal fury. This was one kind of animal that wanted to cut the head off another kind of animal that had invaded its territory. The façade was not there. A rapist dressed as a teacher of English literature was there, who had somehow managed to get into Britain. As Jack left the classroom, not only the eyes of Mr Hussein but also the eyes of every student in the back row followed him out.

Jack took some pleasure in this before realising that causing this scene, this eruption, had done little more than keep him away from Agatha. More than that, it had exposed his loyalty to her in front of Mr Hussein. If anyone were really going to be punished for this, it was, as ever, going to be Agatha. So Jack hated everything. He left the school early, not bothering to sign out, and simply headed through the front door to go out and drink with the old men at The Goat. His victory had been shallow and completely selfish. He had exposed Mr Hussein to a cadre of students, a third of whom already seemed to know the kind of man that he was and supported him for ethnic reasons, and two-thirds of whom were already partly intimidated by him. Well, Jack considered, maybe he had made two or three English students realise who the man was. But it wasn't worth the toll on Agatha. She would suffer anyway. But now she would suffer Mr Hussein's anger at him; she would suffer additionally, he told himself as his madness dropped away into fear.

Jack pressed the green button by the automatic door near the reception desk. The trick to leaving early was just not to draw attention to yourself. He said nothing. He stood officially. The receptionist seemed not to notice. He left through the still-opening automatic door. A pigeon cooed in a birch tree by the old manor and the graffiti of the student in the blazer.

Jack passed the same streets, the same dismal church, walked over the same mutating cobblestone and wood, went down the same passageway, analysed the homeless tents to find the previously arranged needles missing, and exited the underpass to find no mother and daughter out on the path. The brown tower extending far over the pub had a squatter smoking a spliff out of one of its broken windows, a hole right in the middle of the building's face. Jack didn't remember the window's being broken before. Yet he didn't focus on this for long, because he quickly became aware of a more important change. This time, he supposed since he was early, there was a long queue of robed Muslim women waiting to get into the mosque at the bottom of the road. Opposite the pub, at an Arab family restaurant not previously open, a conflagration of young men was gathered speaking in Urdu and pointing at the entrance of The Goat. Jack didn't know why. Their voices were brotherly and mocking rather than disrespectful.

Here was the Muslim thirty to thirty-five per cent of Bothelford gathering to listen to their Imam. Jack looked again. No— it wasn't all of them. It was mainly the women, many of them heavily pregnant. Whatever blessings they had come to receive were, in all likelihood, dedicated to fertility. The men at the restaurant were probably their husbands then, Jack thought. He didn't want to acknowledge it, but the entire scene felt tacitly threatening. He didn't feel at home and, in truth, he wasn't at home. It wasn't his home anymore; it was somewhere different. Jack had never seen a number of self-conscious white people organised in the same way. He decided to enter The Goat, which, by all appearances, the husbands were laughing about. Jack wondered if maybe they were laughing at it just because it looked derelict and represented what was happening generally all over Britain.

But then it turned out that that wasn't it, or that wasn't *just* it, because when Jack swung the pub door open on its weak, gold-painted hinge, he knew straight away what the cause of the men's laughter had been. Perhaps in different circumstances, Jack too would have laughed. For it was Basil Alawi. He was sitting there at the bar wearing a garish, three-piece suit and drinking what looked like an extremely expensive bottle of red wine. The Ulster-Scotsman was sleeping in the corner on a leather chair, a box of cigarettes in hand. The barman was an automaton like before. He experimented with the coffee machine that never worked. He took a key out of a pink, clay pot with a hippo on the side and used it to open a box of rat poison by the fridge.

Jack looked again at Basil. He was dressed—Jack searched for a simile—like a pimp. He was drinking; he was a member of a minority sect; and he was dressed like a cheap pimp by mistake. That was why the men opposite were laughing. Basil didn't look drunk. But Jack observed that his bottle was already half empty and his glass was an orb of deep red. In the months that Jack had not seen him, Basil had grown a small, neat moustache. The highest compliment Jack could give him was that he looked vampiric. His lips were stained from swallowing down a prior glass.

Basil smiled at Jack with a mouth full of teeth. He shivered. 'Jack, my friend. Come sit with me.'

Jack searched for things to say that would keep him from attacking Basil.

'I didn't think Muslims were supposed to drink,' said Jack.

Basil pulled out a stool with a red seat cover for Jack to sit on. '*Ala*', said Basil, calmly. '*-wite*; I'm an Alawite.'

Jack cracked his knuckles lightly but decided to sit. The barman automatically presented him with an empty glass.

'You didn't think I was allowed to drink, eh? Well, I didn't think that sixteen-year-olds were allowed to drink in this country,' Basil said.

'Others have broken the law in worse ways,' said Jack.

Basil looked straight ahead at the mirror behind the bar as the barman poured Jack a drink from the bottle. Basil gulped down most of his glass, and the barman refilled it.

'Another one,' Basil said to the barman. 'Another bottle, sir. I can tell we're going to be sitting here for some time.' He half-turned to Jack, although he wasn't speaking to him at all: 'Claret?'

Jack didn't answer.

'Claret, it is.'

The barman brought it, plunged a bottle opener into it, and pulled the cork up and out.

'*Also*—' Basil said, dropping a fifty-pound note down on the bar in front of him; he addressed the barman. 'We would like to speak in private. It is important, friend. Buy yourself some lunch in the meantime.'

Not reluctantly, the barman took the money and got a pack of cigarettes from under the bar. The barman looked at Basil. He barely raised an eyebrow when Basil replied: 'No, not for *that* ....'

Then the barman nodded. He got up and left and slammed the door behind him. Beyond it, briefly, Jack glimpsed the swelling crowds of Muslim men waiting to collect their wives halfway down the street. This was just for one Imam, Jack thought. What about the other four? How many of these people actually lived in Bothelford? But then Basil wanted them to cheers.

Jack hesitated; he raised his glass with Basil. It was a sign of respect he shouldn't have bothered to give before the argument began.

NINE

There was a twist in Jack's stomach that did not easily loosen. It hurt. The air in the pub was filled with a light dust that tasted sharp on Jack's tongue, like fragmented glass. He hadn't noticed it when he had come to The Goat before, possibly because he hadn't previously had any intention of speaking. But now, today, he faced his opponent and tried to overlook his silly costume. What else could he focus on? Basil's eyes were slightly red around the edges; there was a deep pain but no embarrassment that dwelled within them. These were the eyes of someone who had never cried in his life and yet had deeply, sorely wanted to. The light above the bar was shaped like a heart with an arrow going through it, and it cast a red glow over both of them.

Jack drank. Basil drank.

'So, you're angry with me,' said Basil. 'Because I'm dating Agatha.'

'She told me that you were in love with her, and that Mr Hussein was too.'

'He is. I am not; I am doing my duty.'

Jack inspected Basil's face. They didn't look directly at each other but talked past each other. Jack could tell Basil was being serious, whatever he meant by duty.

'Agatha told me that you raped her and Mr Hussein raped her and potentially others raped her. She showed me the missing tooth in the middle of her face. She took my Cipralex.'

'Did you sell them?' said Basil.

'What?'

'Did you sell her Cipralex tablets?'

'Stop changing the subject.'

'I am not changing the subject,' said Basil. 'Context is important.'

'Contextualise whether you … did *that* to Agatha, then.'

'She and I are lovers, certainly,' Basil said, drinking. 'We are boyfriend and girlfriend.'

Jack didn't know how to deal with this calmness. With embarrassment, with denial, with guilt, he could deal, but not this. Was Basil simply going to explain how everything he had done was justified, instead of even bothering to deny it?

'*But she's*—' said Jack.

'And how old do you think I am?' said Basil. 'Look at my face again.'

Jack turned and observed him. This Syrian face, until now unnoticed, bore the signs of either a hair transplant or a series of Botox injections. Yes, it surgically approximated the face of a teenage boy, and yet it couldn't have belonged to one. The moustache somehow made this all obvious now.

'On another issue, have you ever seen my parents, Jack?'

'No.'

The face grinned softly; it was a handsome face.

'If you had seen them, Jack, you would understand the point I am trying to make. My father was thirty-five when he was introduced to my mother, and she was fourteen. I am the product of their marriage. For me, for my family, this is an historical norm. For Westerners also, it was an historical norm, until very recently.'

Jack was watching the counter, the decorative postcards of women posing with cocktails. He couldn't stand Basil's face.

'The Greeks,' said Basil. 'They married girls according to the same procedure. So did the Prophet, although that will mean little to you. What is not an historical norm is how you Westerners now pursue women. That is very much not normal at all.'

'Then was it', said Jack, rigid, 'the historical norm for your father to *share* your mother with other, older men? Because you are sharing Agatha, apparently.'

Basil laughed just lightly enough that he avoided getting a glass in the face.

'It is a certain tradition; this tradition is referred to sometimes as *taharrush gamea*. It is appalling; it is for the peasants. They go up to the women; they surround the women—' Basil could see that Jack was getting volcanically angry.

'Rest assured, however, I would never support or participate in anything like that. That is the domain of Abdul Hussein. He and his brother, his brother having many wives already, and yet an appetite, they are the ones to condemn. I am working against them.'

'They raped Agatha.'

'It is indeed terrible.'

'You raped Agatha.'

'I am going to marry her,' said Basil.

Whether it was the strange glassy air, Jack couldn't tell. He tasted something. Black bile.

'Her time in this world has been terrible ... and not, purely, due to the crimes of Muslims.'

Jack imagined a great dark fabric, almost veil-like, sweeping back. One of his organs hurt, but he couldn't tell which one.

'What are you talking about, Basil?' he said.

He was involuntarily grinding his teeth when Basil produced his iPhone, which had a case decorated with the Union Jack. 'I am sorry for explaining so slowly,' said Basil. 'Did Agatha ever tell you about her mother?'

'No.'

'You must promise me that you will not hit me, and I will show you something. Do you promise?'

'I ... *promise*,' said Jack, achingly.

'All right then. Jack, this is Mrs Darger. You must know that I do not consider her type to be women at all. This is a cultural distinction.'

Jack bent, and saw, and wretched, and looked again. It was a naked blonde woman posing with what looked like a plastic black penis in her mouth. She had the phrase 'Black Cock Slut' painted over her exposed breasts as she sucked it.

'She is wearing the underwear of a young girl,' said Basil. 'I do not know whether they are Agatha's.'

'Get that the fuck out of my sight.'

'OK. Please just don't hit me. Try to understand.'

'Get that the *fuck* out of my sight!' said Jack. He got up. He took Basil by the collar of his jacket, and he could tell that Basil was terrified. 'What is she, some prostitute or something? You think that makes it all right to do that to Agatha?'

Basil shook his head. 'I will ... explain,' he said.

Jack turned to see the Ulster-Scotsman shaking a little in his sleep at the back.

'We do not want him to wake up,' Basil said.

'*Explain*,' said Jack.

Basil sighed, and drank, and spluttered a little.

'That woman, Mrs Darger,' he said, 'is an OnlyFans model. That website: you pay women to do porn, any porn you like. I do *not* watch porn.'

Jack could feel now, for the first time, how much larger he was than this man, this nineteen, or twenty, or twenty-three-year-old man named Basil Alawi. He was tall for his age, but he hadn't before experienced the advantage of height and natural strength over another man.

'There is a group chat. Maybe she has even told you. It is called *white tings*, in lower case.'

'Yes,' said Jack.

'It is the OnlyFans model group chat. But for the owners. The owners of the camera technology, and, to be frank, they are the owners of the women. They collected Mrs Darger some years ago.'

'... You mean to say there's a porn network in this town ... that lures women into itself ... and—'

'They are trying to *branch out*, Jack Grundon. They are trying to get younger girls. Do you know what I am saying?'

Jack suddenly, horrifically knew.

'They are trying to *get* Agatha. Do you understand?' said Basil. 'I know who these men are. Mr Hussein makes me want to vomit, but he is just a handler. These men, these men are truly terrible. They will hurt Agatha, and they will hurt Mrs Darger—they will kill them, maybe, unless they get the young girl in some videos.'

Jack was silent.

'They will say she is small for her age. They will say she is eighteen. She will not be. This has happened on Pornhub before. You know, they take the young girl, and they make her act and dress up.'

Was it odd that Jack's limbs were twitching? Should he be concerned that his legs seemed to want to jump up at the bar?

'*I am going to marry her*,' said Basil. 'I am going to marry her because your police do *nothing*. I am going to arrange a wedding ceremony with her. We will veil her. We will keep her from these people. My father and my mother, all are agreed. We can't take what is happening to the girl. The police do nothing for her. Her mother does not care for her. Mrs Darger, the mother, she does not care!'

Jack was not biting his nails but, once more, lightly stripping the skin from the top of his right thumb. Part of him wanted to know how deeply he could get into it before he reached the bone. He felt a heavy soreness. He clasped the lobe of his right ear repeatedly. He blew his nose in a black napkin on the bar. Basil brought up his phone again and showed Jack, at a distance, a video this time: 'Does this look like a woman who cares for her daughter? Yet you accuse *me*—'

Without looking at the video, only hearing Mrs Darger's moans, Jack snatched Basil's iPhone out of his hands, and then he smashed it. He smashed it against the bar. He smashed it seven times. He utterly destroyed the dented black screen, and then he trampled it under his feet. He got the Union Jack phone case in his hands, and he ripped the cover off it.

Jack spoke automatically, '*I am accusing you of raping a teenage girl because she told me you raped her, and I believe you have, and I want to hear what you have to say in defence.*'

Basil was silent.

'You haven't denied it,' said Jack. 'Are you going to deny it?'

'We have had sex, yes.'

Jack said: 'How?'

Basil responded: 'She met me in the local library. She said I looked sensitive. She invited me to her room after school. She had been revising for school exams. I was not at the school at the time. Then Mr Hussein—he is a family friend—permitted me to sit in her classes. I am also small for my age. I could pass.'

'*But she was ...*'

'She invited me back to her house, then to her room to get away from Mrs Darger; (I noticed then the inside of her hips). The entire bottom section of the house is a photography studio. I do not lie. I never lie, Jack. They film in there in that house, the owners, the owners of the women. The police do nothing. The police know about it. I have seen an officer make requests of Mrs Darger when she is doing the porn. She does anything because she cannot refuse. They beat her. For Agatha, she does not care.'

Jack didn't know what he was going to do to him. Was he even being honest? Was that really how it had happened, the sex? Jack didn't believe it. But, nevertheless, the way Basil explained things, there was nothing that could be done now. There was nothing that could be investigated. There was no way he could prevent Agatha's 'abuse', although that term was a shoddy euphemism for what had happened and was going to keep happening. What could he or Agatha *actually* do? At best, according to Basil, she could select a slightly gentler rapist, namely himself.

'It is in the centre of the town,' Basil said. 'It is opposite St Michael's. Medium-size house.'

In his mind, Jack could see it vividly. He could see the white walls, the creeping vines outside. The house was at least three hundred years old. The bricks were disordered, but rustic. Before Bothelford became an industrial town, it was there. Now its bottom floor was being used as a porn studio.

Basil said, 'The boys in her English class ...'

'Classes are different now. It's A Levels.'

'Ah, then Jamal and Mohammad and—I think—there are some younger and older ones; there is a boy Ali in particular, he is looking forward to seeing her, to seeing Agatha.'

Jack searched his memory for the name Ali. He had definitely heard of an Ali before, maybe years ago, but he couldn't recall where from.

'Some of these boys are younger than you, smaller,' said Basil. 'One of them is nine. You are sixteen. Much younger, a child to you. They have met Agatha. They have seen her blonde hair. *Please don't hit me.* They circulate about her in the playground sometimes, and she thinks they are innocents. But they are looking forward to seeing her fucked on the group chat. They are all on the group chat. This is the *white tings* group chat. It is the same with this other girl—'

'Jessie ...'

'Yes, that is her name, Jack Grundon. She is even younger.'

'Are you thinking of marrying her too?'

'Ah, that is too young for me,' said Basil, grinning sadly. 'But maybe there are others, others who could save her. ...'

Jack hit Basil in the face. The blow landed perfectly between his eyes, shattering his glasses completely, and causing the smashed frame to actually go up *into* Basil's right eye. The cracked black frame was suddenly crushed up into his pupil, widening the hole along with several squares of glass. Basil somehow still managed not to fall; all his pain went directly into rage.

'I can't see! I can't see!!' Basil said, screaming. 'I curse you! I curse Agatha! I curse you, by Allah; I curse you!'

Basil was too weak to fight, and yet he cursed vibrantly.

'You are dogs, you English! Your women are whores. Your girls are easy pickings, and we are picking. We are *picking* them. It can-*not* be averted, Jack Grundon!'

'Then tell me why,' said Jack; Jack was surprised at himself for asking this, for pausing whilst Basil sat there, and just bled.

Time froze. Basil bled. He simply bled. The Ulster-Scotsman snored.

'Because,' Basil said, spitefully sucking the pain down into his lungs as Jack threatened to hit him. 'Your race conquered our race; with Syria, it was mainly France, but it was your white race all the same. Your white race humiliated India and Pakistan and Syria and Africa, though they too were our slaves, yet we are beyond them! We are beyond them, but you white men have made us feel as they do, giving your gifts, your tools, your humiliations to all in common. Do you not understand me, Jack? We the non-white, we the collectively colonised had no such tools! We varied immensely, but now we are all one in a global struggle because you took, and then you gave them! What has become of this? We have our own militaries, yes. And we do not need you. We can rise. But I ask you, I ask you ... with these tools, what has become of us?'

Basil ripped a square of glass from out of the top of his right eyelid, almost yelled, but channelled the pain he felt into a groan. He was eloquent and bleeding, shivering from the top of his face. Petals of blood scattered on his chest as the square came out. When he spoke this time, although Jack couldn't know this, all his faith in being rescued by the men outside had vanished. He felt himself already at Jack's mercy for he was already bleeding. In blood, he darkened.

'I think ... there is not a boy in Syria, Afghanistan, and so on ... who does not go to sleep without dreaming of the face of a white whore. He sees them on the phone, the white phone, do you know what this means, Jack? He is tempted.

He is destroyed. His wife looks inadequate. He hungers for the white people who have destroyed him and who have allowed themselves to be destroyed. Thousands destroyed, thousands and thousands destroyed, and offering girls to him like mangoes; they are so stupid! More stupid than blacks, more stupid than chickens. What did my father say?' Basil's eyes looked strange as he stared ahead of him and tried to remember, and Jack wondered what visions he was seeing. 'My father said, "These chickens let the fox into the henhouse and shun the farmer for wanting to keep them safe!" Ha, well, I am one of a billion foxes, Jack, one of several billion. I am the great fox who says that such chickens deserve to die. Such men as are led by women and give us, their humiliated enemy, everything they have, they deserve to be fucked and to die. It is an historical process! The white man had his turn in the sun, and now he turns his back on it, giving it—in fact—to us, now we shall make him know us! The fox, he is let in as a guest but laughs because he knows he remains a fox!—' Basil grinned when he saw Jack's damp irises; he spoke in a waltzing joy. 'There is your answer. Because you do not fight back, we know you deserve all that comes.'

Jack nodded, sighed, breathed. He saw red. He shoved Basil off of his chair. He watched him fall. Then Jack said, coolly, though mad, 'If it's an historical process that cannot be averted,'—he was suddenly on the verge of crying—'*this* is too, and *this*, and *this*.' He kicked Basil in the genitals repeatedly as he screamed.

Jack knew that this was selfish, violent, not good. Would it even help Agatha? Why was this violence necessary? Basil had told him everything, almost everything! Yet Jack kept kicking him. As Basil screamed his curses, the Ulster-Scotsman at the back of the pub awakened and burst into insane laughter at the mutilated Arab on the floor. Jack didn't mean to cut into Basil's eyes, and yet he had. He had. He regretted it. But he had. This was the new world. This was the world in which Jack Grundon had permanently, ragingly blinded an Arab man in one eye. He couldn't excuse himself. Jack especially couldn't excuse himself because the man he had attacked was an Arab, because of the legions of men waiting outside as Basil, their brother, yelled.

Basil tried to get up, but he collapsed into the side of the bar, and the wine bottle they had been drinking dropped and smashed on the floor right next to his face.

'I am going to *curse* you!' said Basil. 'May your mother be turned into a kafir whore! May you rot in jail! May you be raped in jail, Jack Grundon!'

Jack kicked him really hard, one more time, and then Basil was quiet. He wasn't dead, but quiet. Jack realised then that he was not going to go to Cambridge. He realised he would not return to school. He realised either he would go to prison, face the Muslim men outside, escape only to be found again by them, or die. Would he kill himself to escape? What would happen when the barman came back? His future suddenly ceased to exist. A black diamond appeared underneath his feet, or it felt like one did.

Jack stumbled over Basil and was about to open the door when he felt an intense pain in his foot, then his ankle. Could it have been a piece of glass? He looked down and saw Basil trying to stab him with the shattered edge of the wine bottle. It went in. A great pyramid protruded from his left ankle, from his sock. It felt like the mouth of a rottweiler had closed on it. A piece of flesh was flapping loose from that area, even poking out underneath the sock. Yet Jack was so filled with adrenaline that it didn't matter, couldn't matter in comparison to what he knew was coming. He shouted as he pulled his leg free and shambled to the exit. He swung the door open. The barman wasn't back yet. Basil had caught him in the ankle, but the barman wasn't back yet!

Sunlight erupted potently through the door as Jack shuffled through and out of The Goat. He passed the Arab men at the restaurant. They stopped laughing, asked him (‘*Habibi!*’) if he wanted assistance; their hostility didn't come quickly enough to destroy him. He had to go.

‘No,’ Jack said. ‘I've got to get home. I've got to see my mother. My mother!’

The ground was dull, and grey, and concrete as ever. The birds were ugly. The Arab women remaining were frightened by Jack, he could tell, as blood trailed from his ankle. His sight blurring gradually, he moved as rapidly as he could. At the end of the street was the war memorial. This would be the last time he passed it, he knew, because his life was over. Could Basil arrange for him to be gang raped in prison? It was possible. Jack lightly wept not from any pain but from the realisation, once more, that he had just ruined his own life.

No one sat at the war memorial this time. Neither Arab man nor woman used it as a stool. He struggled on. It was an absolutely beautiful day. The blue sky was the colour of his own eyes, and he felt a surging kinship with every bird and bush in his vicinity, even as he vividly imagined himself hanging from the bar above his mother's kitchen, what punishments would be meted out to Agatha for his outburst. Blood formed thousands of shapes within his brain. Yet he had the strangest impression that the gods were smiling at him, and he had always been exactly where he needed to be, not Cambridge, not some university, but right here, right now, in Bothelford.

After half an hour of stumbling, occasionally spinning around to check if anyone was following him, and stopping in public bathrooms to inspect his wound—(tear out the deeply-rooted, glass shards)—he came upon the beautiful hill on which he lived, mourned for the life he had had, and regretted his moronic mistake. He told himself then he was a fool. But as if it were itself a stained-glass window, the whole house suddenly radiated with the sun behind it. The gardens swelled with vines. His heart pulsed maniacally. The imaginary diamond he had felt surge under his feet expanded into a black cube with white gold at the edges. He stared at the land. The scene before him looked as it would have—Jack knew; he didn't dream, he knew—five hundred or even six hundred years ago! It was an old sun in splendour, and before it, he was dragging his tattered, wretched leg. He was stamping blood up the garden path.

He stumbled to the wooden front door of his own home and heard bird calls, blackbirds and wrens. He considered their own thousand-year-old tradition of songs. He knocked; Mary Phillips appeared in a sundress with no phone. He dropped into her arms.

TEN

After the tattered clothes and home surgery, after the ripping out of glass and washing of ankles, after the yells and panting of his mother, before the coming day, before the flashing sirens of the police and media, before the articles written about him and what he had done, the sentence that was surely waiting for him, Jack went to sleep as deeply as he could. He took three Cipralex tablets before bed. His mother hugged him, cursed him when he explained a fraction of what had happened. He stayed there. His father came. He wept. All passed quickly. Jack tried to fall asleep so deeply that he wouldn't wake. He tried to find a doorway out of a dream; there must be such a thing. He tried to convince himself to believe there was such a thing. He slept as the sun went red, but he didn't feel entirely asleep. There was a female presence across the room he knew. The sun was such a bright red, and so close he felt it was watching him alone. His clothes were white. Now there was a dark presence across the room. She thrust herself upon him. Now there were two of them. One of them said that he, Jack, was chosen, and the other one said that she was coming back. He felt the green-eyed one reach into his intestines. He recalled the name Marine Emery.

Jack woke up. Had a day gone by? Had two days? Three? Five? Jack panted the continuation of whatever words he had yelled in his dreams to the yellow jackets that, waking, he saw sitting there at the end of his bed.

'I am Officer Fahir,' said a voice. This was a real voice. 'I am glad to finally have your attention.'

Whatever happened next passed so quickly, or so slowly, it felt like a dream, although it couldn't have been a dream. The next two weeks of Jack's life consisted of his effectively turning off his brain and saying the words 'Yes' and 'No'. Almost nothing else besides that came out of his mouth in that time, and when, on occasion, he was asked to provide something more substantial, he experienced a deeper agony than he knew was possible. Officer Fahir politely explained that they were investigating him for a racially motivated attack against Basil Alawi and for selling drugs to Agatha Darger. There was something else that he was accused of, also, but Officer Fahir didn't want to acknowledge what it was in front of Jack's parents in case it destroyed not only them but, more importantly, the suspect psychologically. He said to Jack that he appreciated that this was not easy news to hear. Jack nodded like a mannequin, as perhaps he only could, but saw around the mouth of Officer Fahir such deep pride. It was perhaps the same pride he had noticed on the lips of Mr Hussein.

Jack wolfed his Cipralex down whenever it was available, although Officer Fahir stopped him the first time, saying that Jack wasn't allowed to take anything without his permission. He said he didn't want Jack to 'do anything stupid'. Well, Jack wasn't going to do *that!* But the fact that Officer Fahir expected him, a sixteen-year-old boy, to do so implied a lot about what Fahir and the state had planned for him. Jack sulked and worried.

From Mary Phillips's house, Jack, Officer Fahir, and his deputy Lauren pulled away and left in a police car; Jack wasn't cuffed. He collaborated, understanding that there was nowhere to go. He sat in the back seat of Officer Fahir's police car as it drove past the hill, through the centre of Bothelford, and beyond St Michael's. But as they passed that church, and therefore opposite the front window of Mrs Darger's house, Jack glimpsed what looked like a Syrian boy with a white eyepatch sitting opposite a crying blonde girl. What was happening? In his darkest fantasies, Jack knew what was happening. He got a chill. He guessed at the substitution that had been planned, that Basil was in his place and he was in Basil's.

That night, he slept for the first time in a holding cell by himself. The windows were barred. The bunk bed was cold, and he banged his head on the ceiling when he woke up. The woman at the reception desk had been kind and accommodating. She had treated him as if he were there merely for a school visit. She could not imagine what he had been accused of. The alternative was that she actually liked Jack because she knew he was meant to have done something terrible. Such women, Jack imagined, go to work in police stations like this one. By the same woman, Jack's phone was confiscated from him, but not before he checked his phone and found dozens of posts that were talking about him. He was glad he didn't have to look in more detail; at least he had been cared for in those terms, kept from most of what was occurring. It didn't last.

The next morning under a sky that was as beautiful as the one on the previous day, although Jack could observe it only every so often, he was told that Agatha Darger had accused him of rape and sexual assault, that he would be interrogated imminently about this, and that the consequences for his behaviour would be determined in a courtroom sooner rather than later. Jack spent the whole day in a daze, estimating the pain Agatha had been subjected to, whatever it had taken to make her lie. But what did it matter? What did anything matter? Jack had been killed. He had fallen lower than he had ever expected for the sake of violence he knew he could have expressed heroically in any other age. But not this age. This age was his enemy. If he were the enemy of this age, what had he done to become its enemy? Maybe he deserved it.

That afternoon, he was visited by an 'internet expert' from Prevent and told that they had gone through his laptop, that they had found extracts of schoolwork by him on the novel *Disgrace*, and that this book had rape as a central theme.

'Were you inspired by this book, Jack?' said the expert.

'It's an A Level text.'

The woman interrogating him was fat and wore expensive, red boots. Her eyes narrowed with fury and joy.

'That doesn't answer my question, Jack.'

'No, I wasn't inspired by it then.'

Jack noticed her face was the same colour as the table he leaned his elbows on.

'You weren't?' she said.

'I think the book is horrible, and I don't know why the class made us read it.'

'Do you find it horrible because there are black men in it having non-consensual sex with a white woman?'

Images came into the mind. He looked at the grey window behind her, the dark wall, then the carpeted floor with clumps of hair sticking out of it.

'Partly.'

The expert bit her lip on the left side. She stiffened.

'You said on your blog—I quote,' (it was very clear to Jack that she loved saying, 'I quote') "I am a hated minority in my classroom and soon I will be a hated minority throughout what was once my country. I suppose that this is what counts as modern education: education for the world to come."

'... Yes?' said Jack. 'What's incorrect about that?'

The expert looked at him, and nodded, and made a note. No discussion was necessary. All she had to do was check the boxes on the form in front of her: a well-paid, easy job. She grinned as she turned the page, and Jack got the idea that what he was looking at was a kind of android with a red ring of lipstick around its mouth and that she was trying, above all, to obey her programming—to not laugh evilly, directly in his face. This was especially hard for her to do when she asked her favourite question.

'Are you a racist, Jack?'

Now it was Jack's turn to stiffen. Rather than take too long to answer, he decided he would give his first, most honest, instinctive reaction.

'... I don't ... know. ...'

Again, she wrote down a few sentences on her clipboard.

'Agatha was being assaulted by Mr Hussein, by Basil Alawi. They're a gang,' said Jack.

'Speak to Officer Fahir about this,' said the expert.

'Why?'

'It's outside my expertise.'

She closed her clipboard and got up and left, having acquired all that she needed. 'Well, that was horrible,' Jack thought. Clearly, he had presented the wrong answer, which was the true one. In his mind, Jack recollected that the correct answer and the true one had differed in almost every academic situation he had ever been in, excluding most Maths and Physics lessons. And why was that? Meanwhile, Jack was left in the bland office for an hour and played with a rubber band he had found under the table. Little moments like this were worth enjoying. He twisted the red band around his thumbs and fingers. He was offered a coffee by Officer Fahir. He was given a copy of the Bible—if he wanted to read it—by the priest Oliver Turner, who came to visit him once and never again. They also had a conversation. But it was so empty of meaning that it isn't worth repeating. In the meantime, Jack played with the red rubber band. It wasn't that Oliver Turner didn't like Jack or didn't believe that Jack was innocent but that the cost he, Oliver, would have to endure for defending Jack was just too great, that made him spout nonsense and drivel. Especially as a priest, a profession maligned since the Catholic Church's sexual-abuse scandal, Oliver couldn't afford to be a friend to Jack Grundon, the accused. He couldn't, it seemed, even allow himself to think that that was a possibility. So, 'Oh well,' thought Jack.

Nevertheless, during their interaction, Jack remembered a story that Oliver had once told him about the Athenian plague. He remembered it by gazing into the man's familiarly coffee-stained mouth. It was meant to have been mentioned at the end of a book that Jack hadn't read called *On the Nature of Things*, which was by a Roman author. Yet the Athenian plague hadn't been like the Chinese virus; it wasn't something that you could just isolate yourself from or recover from. Families struggled through burning wreckage to ceremonially bury their dying and dead ancestors before succumbing to the plague themselves and then required their own younger relatives to bury them on top of that. This often occurred whilst the mourners fought with others trying to secure funeral plots for their own dead. Some philosophers had apparently interpreted the story as the insertion of a Christian monk years after the book had been written to try to make the Epicureanism it advocated, or the idea of living the good life without an afterlife, totally invalid. Jack didn't know about any of this. What he knew was that he felt like he had contracted the Athenian plague, and even those who loved him, even those who cared about him as a student or a friend, couldn't come near him, or they too would grow sick with it, succumb, die alone.

The only exception to this rule, it turned out, was Fauna
Williams, who, inexplicably and perhaps due to his sick attrac-
tion to Jack, wrote him a short letter as soon as the news got
out about what he had been accused of and spread like wild-
fire over the whole school. The letter arrived in a yellow enve-
lope two weeks after Jack had entered the holding cell. It was
brought to him by his own mother, who now did not speak
to him, Agatha's accusation having torn up most of the bond
between her and her son. She closed the door serenely.

Jack looked at the letter, which was the colour of a weak
flame. It was like the woman hadn't even been in the room, let
alone been any relative of his. Jack opened the letter and was
surprised to find a featureless pale blue card with no kisses, no
romantic drawings, which he already knew Fauna was more
than capable of.

Dear Jack,

> *I am sorry about the way I have treated you.*
> *Given where you are, this probably means very little*
> *to you right now. But I wanted to say it regardless,*
> *because I feel like I have partly contributed to your*
> *situation. When I used a different name, Agatha*
> *Darger once came to me and told me about what hap-*
> *pened to her, and I did nothing at all. She might have*
> *mentioned me by my deadname: Frederick Williams.*
> *Sorry.*

Jack jostled through his memories and recalled the names that Agatha had listed on the day of her confession, those she had asked for help from previously. Now that he thought about it, Agatha had mentioned a Frederick.

I want you to know, Jack, that I did nothing. Perhaps this is because I am smarter than you, but I have the sneaking suspicion it is because I'm a coward. I am a woman now, and yet I still understand the value of bravery. When Agatha told me about the gang, about her mother, I didn't fight anyone. I didn't go to the police. I knew that if I did, what would happen to me is very clearly what is currently happening to you. I will speak to Agatha when I see her next because I think she appreciates all your efforts.

She appreciates you in all the ways that she has come to revile me.

Yes, I am probably going to get into Cambridge for all the reasons that you aren't, but that is only because failures of courage are rewarded in today's world.

I do not know if you believe in God, Jack. But I want you to know that I think he loves you and one day I will regret everything I have done, and you will regret nothing.

Jack was too numb to laugh, yet he grinned a tiny grin: Fauna, the Christian?

Perhaps I am speaking out of character and allowing my old ways to affect me more than they should. I am the 'Woke' one, after all. But rest assured, I do not believe any of these accusations, and whatever happens, the scandal, the self-hatred that you currently feel will one day go away.

I am sorry that all I can tell you is to 'sit tight', Jack. But you have inspired me to help you, and I am going to do something, whatever I'm capable of doing.

—Did you know my mother is Vice-President of the National Education Union?

(I am also very big on Instagram.)

Love,
Fauna

None of this, in all likelihood, would work. But it wasn't nothing. Jack felt like just a little bit of air had been let out of him, that he was no longer in danger of bursting spontaneously into fire. Fauna, it was true, had given him a gift. The world was strange.

ELEVEN

When Jack woke up three mornings later, he heard the unlocking of the door of the holding cell. It wasn't a roommate for him, whom he expected sooner or later would come in to terrorise him, but Officer Fahir. He looked extremely angry but managed, underneath his long black beard, to suppress that emotion to a professional degree. Jack could only imagine what was going to happen as Fahir opened his pocket and provided Jack with his old phone. He sat on the upper bunk bed, dusted his eyes, and saw that on it were messages from Fauna Williams and Basil Alawi.

'Did you ask him to do something?' said Fahir.

'No, I didn't,' said Jack, not really knowing what he was talking about.

'Good.'

Jack looked at the messages, which were already open, and Officer Fahir had clearly already gone through.

'Have you arrested Frederick?' said Jack.

'You mean Fauna?'

'Yes.'

'Why would *we* do that?'

Jack bit his tongue.

'Fauna sent me a letter saying that he was going to try and help me legally.'

'I have read the letter,' said Fahir. 'You can read Fauna's message in your own time. I want you to read Basil's message to me now.'

'Haven't you read it already?'

'Yes, but that isn't what I asked you.'

Jack remembered a few of the interrogation videos he had seen on YouTube and decided to push his luck.

Jack said, 'I don't think I need to answer any questions until I have a lawyer.'

But then, Fahir grinned.

'You are going to read the message.'

'Why?'

'Because I am not asking you as a policeman,' said Fahir.

What did Fahir's face remind him of? It was cartoonish.

'Read the message,' said Fahir. 'I dare you not to.'

Jack opened the message from Basil Alawi. It was a sprawling text message, and its anger was palpable. 'Aloud?' said Jack.

'Aloud,' ordered Fahir.

Jack cleared his throat.

'"Dear Jack Grundon, today is the first day ... that I have beaten Agatha."'

Jack winced.

'Keep reading,' said Fahir.

'"Her mother saw me do it. And I would have beaten the woman too if it weren't that she had to be on camera that evening!! I hope you are happy in your cell, Jack Grundon! Do you know why I have been beating Agatha? I have been beating Agatha because I am angry with your disgusting FAGGOT friend Fauna Williams, who filmed me and put it on Instagram. Do you know the humiliation this causes? He has filmed me with his camera. He said that he wanted to speak to the girl's mother about 'sex work and activism'. He is an 'activist' apparently!! He was let in by the stupid white cuntbitch. He waited for her to go to the toilet. He ran to the bedroom. He opened the door. We were found. Agatha unlocked the door. Did she know he was coming? Fauna entered and saw me, and he said, 'How old are you!?' and she screamed her age. And now it is up on the internet. They are METOO-ing me, Jack Grundon. The Kafir whore is METOO-ing me after accusing you. I pray that you are bombarded with nightmares. I am told that we must come and make a deal. Speak to my associate about the deal.'

'What are your thoughts, Jack?' said Fahir.

'He's a dramatic writer.'

'It is a dramatic subject,' said Fahir. 'Tell me what you expect from this deal.'

A wren had landed at the barred windows and was screeching. It flew away.

Jack shivered a little. 'Are you asking me as a police officer,' he said, 'or as an associate of Basil Alawi?'

Fahir looked like he was enjoying himself immensely. Maybe the loyalty between him and Basil was weak. Maybe this was because Basil was an Alawite and Fahir was a Pakistani.

'Answer,' said Fahir.

Jack thought. He pulled the skin under his mouth. He inspected Fahir's body for the sign of bulges, for the sign of knives.

He was about to speak when Fahir said, '*Be realistic.*'

'I want Agatha to be free.'

'Uh-huh.'

'I want Basil and everyone else to leave her alone for good.'

Fahir nodded and made a checking motion on an imaginary clipboard.

'What about yourself, my man?'

'I ...'

'You already know what you want.'

'I don't want to go to prison,' said Jack. 'I want my name cleared.'

'What if you could *just* choose one?'

Jack noticed that Fahir's teeth were so yellow they looked like string cheese.

'I ... don't want to go to prison.' Jack imagined what would happen to him in there and how the gangs would treat him, use him up.

'You will not be able to go back to school. You will never be able to go to university,' Fahir said. 'Do you know what we are going to have to do?'

Jack shook his head.

'We are going to have to investigate and prosecute Basil Alawi. He is unimportant. He said he wanted to 'save' this girl. But he took her all the same. Other than that, things will continue.'

Jack nodded robotically.

'You are not going to go to prison. You are going to go some-where that is like prison but isn't prison. Your reputation—we will do nothing to repair it. Understood?'

'Yes.'

'Yes, what?'

'Yes, sir.'

'There is another side to this discussion, however,' said Fahir. 'You must—' he drew a zip over his mouth. 'About everything. Or Agatha will become the star that so many boys want her to be. And you will go to prison, and things will happen in that prison, as you might have guessed. Is that clear?'

'Yes, sir.'

'This conversation never happened,' said Fahir, happily talking like a TV secret agent.

Yet as he began leaving the room, Jack recalled something else, someone else—the young girl. What was her name? What was the name of the very young girl that Agatha had told him about, who wasn't even in secondary school yet, and yet was being pursued by Muhammad Akbar from his form group?

Her name burst out of Jack's mouth, 'Jessie Waters! But what about Jessie Waters? What's going to happen to her?'

Fahir flipped around and looked at Jack with an animated smile as he stepped through and then began to lock the cell door.

'You didn't ask about Jessie,' said Fahir. 'Enjoy your phone.'

The door closed. Jack was left with all the stories that other people had told about him on social media, a seemingly infinite supply. And then he read over Fauna's message, which was simply, 'Thank me later.' And he didn't know whether to jump for joy or cry.

TWELVE

The next day, Jack got a roommate. He entered the cell as Jack rested. The roommate brought a hammer hidden in his trousers. He was a twitching, balding, drunk man who reminded Jack immediately of the homeless man he had seen so many years ago eat soil. He had tufts of hair that bristled like tufts of grass in a scorched field. He had a tattoo of a dagger on his face that somehow melted and compressed into the skin around his eyelids, dyeing them a permanent black smear. He was Albanian. He was missing three of his fingers due to God knows what. Jack clutched his blanket and pillows in the top bunk for as long as he could.

Once the man's snarling started, it didn't stop. The man waited for him as soon as he needed to go to the toilet in the connected bathroom. Having stayed in so many other cells before, the man considered this bathroom a luxury. He actually grew angry at Jack for not being grateful for having it in a separate room, rather than having to put up with an exposed toilet seat right in the middle of the cell without any walls and with no lockable door. From his bunk, Jack wondered whether to leap down from the hard alloy ladder. But the man pulled him. There would be no heroism. The man got Jack by the collar when he leaned over the side, and then he screamed at Jack his own father's name to make the job easier, and he hit Jack across the forehead with the hammer twice.

Jack wasn't knocked out cold. He felt it. He dropped from the bunk and landed, then the hammer did. The noise was the sound of a pumpkin getting crushed by the wheel of a tractor. Blood shot out. For a minute, Jack lay there, surprised at the special effects that his own body was capable of generating. Then came the pain, the terror. His fear was that the area of his skull that had fractured was going to actively let his brain fluid flow out of it until there wasn't anything left. Jack was suddenly aware that he had a skull and that his brain was in that skull and bashing it meant that he couldn't think as he used to. Where there had been thoughts there was now bone, fragments of bone, and occasional, decorative spurts of his blood. He didn't yell. He gulped. His throat wanted to heave out of the failing assemblage of organs that was now his own cracked head.

Now the man was going to town on the side of the bunk-bed. He was whacking it. He was saying his father's name. He went to the bathroom, and started yelling at his arms where there were black infected needle scars, and yelling at his own reflection, and pulling down his trousers, and pissing all over the place. Jack was just concerned that his head, a chocolate easter egg, he thought, would burst, and the caramel inside of him, his essence, was going to spill all over the floor and then intermingle with the piss. Jack was extremely concerned that now he was retarded. A head wound like that sets you off balance! Jack's head was spinning, and above his front teeth he wondered whether the substance he tasted was leaking out of his head, dripping down from the exposed white stalactite of bone, or whether it was really just spilling forth from his busted, nasal cavity as he hoped. Hoped?

Officer Fahir came and entered with two other officers seemingly as soon as they heard clattering noises from the bathroom: the roommate, whoever he was, smashing up the mirror with the hammer. He was dealt with first, moved to another cell to be by himself, after three or four subduing bashes to his own head with a truncheon. Jack Grundon was left on the floor for a while before the ambulance was called. Fahir did not grace what remained of his sight with anything but a brief thumb's up. Jack's last thought was: 'This was all planned.'

Then he really was out cold. The stars twisted into a fine purple mist. He was subjected to a barrage of hundreds of billions of fluorescent office lights. The upper right quadrant of his skull felt like the wound that the Earth was born out of, or the place where a gigantic, mutant eyeball could expand and grow through, up, out of his own pathetic trounced right eyehole. His parents were alerted that evening. It was urgent, so after being cuffed to his hospital bed, he had to wait only four hours for surgery at Accident and Emergency as opposed to the customary six or eight. Jack didn't hear the word 'fracture' as he slept nor the sound of a drill. Both were used.

The gentle drum of a bone saw he mistook for the dancing feet of a ballerina in a large, oak-panelled room. He had bolts in his head where memories had been. Or it was not that bad. How bad was it then? Jack didn't know, but he would come to believe that his roommate had been hired using heroin by Basil Alawi's connections to attack him, and that this was facilitated by Officer Fahir. That was the end of the story. He had been beaten. The thirsty wolves of social media would have his brains and skull to chew on and his leaky eye socket. They could accuse him of being a predator in the place of Basil as much as they wanted. For he had already been theatrically punished. They could celebrate it! They could beg for his gang rape as much as he supposed Basil and Fahir silently did, and he would still be the dented wreck that he now was. All would understand that an eye had been given for an eye. After the third surgery, Jack perceived an immense shimmering blot that flashed all the colours of the rainbow right in the centre of his vision. He knew what it meant when he saw it. This part of his life, this heroic part of his life, where he fought Basil and tried to save Agatha Darger, was over. Now it was over. And when he awoke in hospital, he was presented with a blue box containing a glass eye. His parents brought a Colin the Caterpillar cake with them to his bedside. His mother sang terribly to drown out everything. It was his birthday. He was seventeen years old.

THIRTEEN

'Phthisis-bulbi,' said the doctor, an hour and a half later. 'in the remaining portions of the eye.'

Jack blushed at these words; he was embarrassed at his own modifications. His eye was white without the glass covering. His hair had turned increasingly grey. The doctor inspected his eye. He was told that his routine was going to change now. Jack's routine each morning would become taking his Cipralex, and then taking a chemical eyedropper, and squeezing it into the whitened husk of a right eyeball that remained before inserting the partial glass eye over it. Then he would take painkillers. When this was first explained to him, he barely processed what the doctor was saying. He absorbed the instructions mechanically instead. He was a kind of machine leaking oil that needed to be tended to delicately. The doctor recommended that he take up a hobby that didn't involve too much thought or concentration. He recommended cable exercises in the gym, the more laborious the better, but not deadlifts. That would take his mind off the pain. It would make him stronger, more confident, despite what had happened. The doctor recommended going on long, lonely walks, and he used the word 'lonely'.

'Better to improve your spatial coordination if you're out by yourself, rather than being puppeted around by Mum and Dad.'

The doctor said this, and Jack did not process it. He recommended coming off the phone. For a plethora of reasons, contact with the school was to be broken off. One of these reasons was that if Jack had any friends there, their reactions to his new appearance in these early healing stages might unsettle him, make him hate himself. Jack heard this. Jack said that his only friend was Fauna Williams, although his mother was surprised that he had never mentioned him before. Jack slipped a black jumper over his head and stood up from his bed, still drugged out of his mind.

'No, Mum. I owe Fauna everything,' he said, pulling the jumper over his neck.

Mary twisted her own greying hair. 'Should we call him here?'

'No,' said Jack. 'I'll see him later. I'll see him when I'm cleared of all charges.'

Mary Phillips looked at Jack's father, confused but also hopeful.

'Trust me,' said Jack. 'All the charges will be dismissed. I am not going to prison, but I'm not going back to school either.'

Mary whispered something to Jack's father.

'Mum, it is *not* the drugs,' said Jack.

'What is it then!?' she shouted. 'How has my baby ended up like this? With a face like ...'.

Jack stared out the window. But there was no view. The glass was too thick for anything but the most mundane light to come in. Jack's father said something to Mary, and she apologised.

'I know what's going to happen,' said Jack. 'It's not good, but it's better than I hoped. At least for me. For others, what's coming is terrible.'

He thought of Jessie. He had no idea how frightening he looked with his white eye, nor noticed the light beard that had grown in over his face. When he left the ward for the police station, he passed a little girl in a strange green and brown outfit in the corridor who passed a little twig into his hands. He had never seen her before. He took it. He took some Cipralex. When he went to sleep that night, the twig was nowhere to be found.

In the morning, in another cell, he applied chemicals to his burning eye. He took his Cipralex. He watched a pornographic recording of an older woman telling him that everything was going to be all right. He washed his hands and read a section from the Gospel of St Matthew, about the Lord's being most pleased with his Son. It was a palliative existence; one recorded in expansions and retractions of pain. Pain was a region, a kind of sub-intellectual continent that shifted over his entire body when some unpredictable, tectonic disruption made it move there. And it could do that whenever it wanted to. It could collapse in on him using whatever fissure it chose. Pain came with stories on the internet about white girls being killed by black drug-dealing boyfriends every other week in the United States, with diagrams published each day that represented the same extinction generally all over the West, with articles about asylum hotels.

Yet pain left Jack, a substantial portion of it, when he was discharged, when whatever sense of duty Officer Fahir felt in keeping his word was expressed. Agatha had been questioned, and she had retracted her accusation, saying that Basil Alawi and others had pressured her into making it. Basil Alawi was soon going to be in custody, wherever he was at the moment, and Fauna's video recording of him was evidence enough of the fact that Agatha was telling the truth. Jack didn't return to school. He went home. For the next month, he was advised to stay in his room, which, having been confined to it over the course of Lockdown, wasn't that difficult for him to accept and endure. Sometimes he would be permitted to go out and pick the litter around the bad side of Bothelford, as pleased both Officer Fahir and—to Fahir's surprise—Jack himself.

Then, that Friday, Jack started the tradition of visiting the pub with his father to talk about how things were going. Many odd looks came Jack's way, presumably due to his appearance, but he didn't care enough to acknowledge them. This pub was different from The Goat; it was called The Two Brewers, and it was close to six hundred years old. The roof of the building was thatched. It was in a nearby village that had once been connected to Bothelford but was at this point surgically separated from it. It was a kind of expensive reservation for the rich English people who could afford in their later years to move out there. It was also the first time, now that he thought about it, that Jack had ever seen families bring their children to a pub. He wondered again if this had been normal once and what had happened to people going out like this in Bothelford, where you couldn't use the toilet in a café without entering a password on the door. Of course, the number of children was disproportionately fewer than Jack had encountered among the Muslims either at school or outside the mosque in Bothelford. But here was a kind of restoration, no matter how small and insignificant it was.

His father gulped down a quarter of his beer glass. He clicked his fingers, Jack thought somewhat rudely.

'We were talking about the local council. ... What do you think is going to happen in the next general election?' said his father.

'Reform will get lots of seats. I don't know if it matters,' Jack stared off into space, trying to remember his train of thought.

'What? How can you say that?' said his father.

'Muslim rape gangs. They will win because people are tired of the Muslim rape gangs.'

'But is that the real reason?'

'Yes.'

'But they weren't all Muslims.'

'A sizeable number of Muslim men are foreigners who are here because they want to fuck white women and then go back to their wives. That's all. They don't understand consent.'

'I really don't like the way you talk about them.'

'OK, I just don't think the fact can be underestimated. The same goes for the fact that whites are going to be a minority in Britain in the next forty years.'

His dad drank his beer, sighed.

'If that's true, why isn't *The Financial Times* talking about it?'

'Look ... I don't think you're ever going to grasp this issue.'

'Tell me why *The Financial Times* isn't talking about it, if it's such an issue?'

'Because *The Financial Times* doesn't want to talk about it, I suppose.'

'You suppose, Jack?'

'How many children does the average Muslim woman have in a lifetime in comparison to the average white woman? I would bet you that the average Muslim woman has three to five, and the average white woman has two or less. We're also still importing these people. How many generations do you think that makes it until they take over our country?'

Jack paused, lowered his voice, as his father's glance implied was the right thing to do. '... *They have already made London a minority white city in a decade and a half.*'

'Jack, why do you have to see this in racial terms?'

Jack cleared his throat. He would respond rapidly; that would carry a punch; it would also mean he could get through this ordeal a little faster.

'Why do I have to see this in racial terms? Because they do. And we do not. And their men regard our women as sex toys. That's why.'

Jack's father was about to leave the table and go to the bathroom. He was upset. He was wondering if Jack's head injury had anything to do with his new political perspectives. The generational gap had evidently deepened, and Jack's father wondered what to do. Maybe if he showed Jack *Roots*, or *Schindler's List*, or any of the great films or TV shows from the nineteen-nineties, Jack would come around, see the horror of what he was saying. Jack's father decided to stay where he was and talk for a bit longer.

'That still doesn't cover the fact neither *The Financial Times* nor *The Economist* have reported on any of these issues,' he said. 'Why haven't they reported on these issues if everything you say is true? And I know it's not; I know personally that you're wrong. But let's pretend you're on point.'

'I don't know,' said Jack, sipping his wine. 'I think that the people who write those papers can't admit that what they believe is wrong. But they all know, deep down, that they are partly responsible for flooding Europe with foreigners who hate us.'

'Really?'

'They know that they encouraged them to hate us. They still encourage hatred and violence against white people by refusing to present ethnic crime data and publish the obvious conclusions that can be made based on the results. They don't do that. They lie. And they say that we are responsible for the behaviour of the migrants because we are oppressors. They go easy on the rapists.'

A woman turned round at the pub table adjacent their one. Jack's father whispered, '*Don't* say ... that word so liberally.'

'It's what's happening. If anyone wants to confront me about it, they can.'

'*People will think you're diminishing the issue.*'

'Ha.'

'What's funny?'

'They are the ones downplaying who's responsible.'

The stare of Jack's white eye was unrelenting. He wondered whether the effect of his Cipralex and the effect of his painkillers were going to be diminished by the alcohol, and then whether he'd have to be rushed to hospital. But those silly thoughts passed.

'I think you need a few lessons about respectability. I'm going to the toilet.'

'I don't care about respectability, and you don't have anything to teach me apart from making money in an economy where AI is going to liquidate your skillset anyway.'

'Fuck off then,' said his father, chuckling.

As Jack's father got up and left to go to the bathroom, the woman at the other table turned around, looked at Jack, and scowled. So Jack smirked, removed his glass eye, and showed her the full extent of his white gaze. She twisted back into her domain. Then he regretted showing her entirely.

Jack sipped his wine. His heart hurt. He wondered whether the joy of frightening this woman was at all akin to the joy that Mr Hussein felt in making Agatha read the passage about rape from the *Disgrace* novel. He didn't know how he felt about seeing Agatha again, despite being prepared to meet Fauna. This was because he absolutely needed confirmation that Officer Fahir and his group were protecting her or simply leaving her alone. Until then, just the thought of seeing her was disturbing. Jack wondered how Agatha's protection would be arranged with Mrs Darger, what kind of alternative work she herself would have to find, or whether she would stay on as an OnlyFans model and prostitute. Jack wondered whether he had been promised anything at all and if he would actually end up getting gangbanged in prison and Basil Alawi would get off scot-free. Even if he were out of prison at the moment, couldn't evidence be doctored? Couldn't lying 'witnesses' be found in the Alawite community?

Jack thought. What was the Arabic term he had read online the other day? Yes, *taqiyya*, the principle of lying to the infidel to conceal your true motives in the name of Allah. Perhaps Officer Fahir had done just that. But if that was the case, why interrogate him at all? Why not simply allow him to be beaten to death without interference? Doubtless, Fauna's footage gave Agatha a kind of confidence to come forward and reveal information to a large audience that she hadn't previously found within herself. And perhaps not just Fahir, and Hussein, and Alawi, but the entire Muslim community in Bothelford was threatened by the revelations that Agatha held within her like a scroll. For if the full, unrestrained truth ever came out, wouldn't a sleeping giant be awakened? Wouldn't the spirits of old England come back to haunt and horrify all those culpable? But Jack didn't know about any of this for certain. He was the only brave Englishman he knew apart from Fauna, and Fauna didn't even identify as a man.

Jack's father emerged from the bathroom. Then he was back outside with a pint for himself and another wine for Jack. Jack looked at the man's slightly pulsing, besuited body, the thin hands, the mildly broken posture, the phone with three tabs from *The Guardian* surely open on it that was tucked into his breast pocket like a chick in its nest.

What data, what articles, what documentaries would be necessary to bring him around to Jack's point of view? Common sense and intuition, Jack knew, wouldn't be enough. He was dealing with the perfect case study of a generation that processed all they knew through the official channels. Alternative opinions were allotted through the same screen, through the same websites. Jack's father would go, and watch, and read, and he wouldn't notice. He had truly never realised that he had only heard from one source his entire life, one screen, and the same four or five presses organised and managed by the same people. No, Jack thought, but that was pushing it too far. Jack remembered that if his dad ever noticed the press ownership, then he noticed Rupert Murdoch, whom the respectable papers despised as a scapegoat for their own corruption and therefore his dad despised also. It was extraordinary, now that Jack thought about it, that this system of censorship and repression had ever worked. How could anyone trust what they had watched or read from only one place or just from the *BBC*, *The Guardian*, and *The Financial Times*, which were all the same, hiring the same staff, airing the same facts? And yet the system had worked. His father had been made into a different kind of person, someone who noticed what he was told to notice rather than deriving anything significant from what was occurring directly before his eyes.

Jack thought and thought. Then there was a vibration in his pocket.

'Might want to check that,' said Jack's father.

Jack turned on his phone and saw that it was a message on Telegram, an app he hadn't used in a very long time. It ended: '... *the clinic.*' Jack opened it and saw the icon of a black anthropomorphic cat with bags under its eyes.

'Sorry, I've got to go to the bathroom.'

'Cheers me first, though,' said his father. 'Bad luck otherwise.'

Jack raised his glass, said cheers, and drank, looking his dad in the eyes. He got up and went through the loose oak door into the pub, cut through the packed interior, brushed past the bar queue, and went to the bathroom. He pissed. He washed his hands. He looked at his white eye in the mirror and put the glass eye back in more comfortably. Then he opened Agatha's message. He went into the toilet cubicle and locked the door. There were a bunch of crossed-out swastikas on the back of the door next to the occasional love heart. He scanned the text. Agatha wrote more lucidly than Jack had ever heard her speak before. She was asking for something serious. He decided to read it all in the locked cubicle.

Jack, since you left school, I'm no longer in Mr Hussein's English class.

I'm only with Miss Lawrence and she is nice to me. I think the Gang has reached an understanding with Mr Hussein and with school. I'm thankful if you had something to do with it.

We're still reading Disgrace, but Miss Lawrence is very good and patient with me. There are bits of the book that I don't like to read. But there was one bit that really interested me. And I'd like to share it with you. I've copied it below. It's about Lucy, the woman who is attacked by the three black men, deciding to keep and love her baby. This is the black baby the men have given her. It's in her womb. She says she's going to keep it in front of her father when he asks her whether she loves the baby yet. When I read this part, I was thinking about myself as Lucy and I was thinking about her father as my dad. Read this.

'All right,' thought Jack.

I am copying the book now:
    'Do you love him yet?' (says David, Lucy's father.)
    Though the words are his, from his mouth, they startle him.
    'The child? No. How could I? But I will. Love will grow—one can trust Mother Nature for that. I am determined to be a good mother, David. A good mother and a good person. You should try to be a good person too.'

Jack read the lines over again. He repeated the phrase *'the child'* in his head, trying to parse its meaning before he continued Agatha's message. He had an inkling of what she wanted to ask him about and what she wanted him to do. He did not want to continue, but he felt he had to.

I think this book and a number of books and films and TV shows that are like it have made it very hard for me to come forward about what's happened. They attack my feelings and they make me feel ashamed

*and stupid for not being able to bear the pain. Enter-
tainment like this makes me feel the right thing to do
is put up with the pain, to understand the culture of
the attackers, to keep quiet because nothing is going to
happen anyway. I've told you this before, haven't I?*

*So then I decided, because I felt stupid and like
I didn't understand what's happened to me, that I
would go and read up about Islam, learn about their
culture, just browse for a little bit. I read parts of the
first surah. I didn't like what I read. I didn't understand it. Then I read parts of another book I randomly
saw in Oxfam. And I liked it. It's Feminist, so maybe
you won't like it. I only read a page but it was interesting. Again, I've copied a bit below to explain my situation. It's important for you to understand me, Jack.*

Jack tried to wipe his eyes and jangled his glass eye by mistake. It hurt. He got a tissue, and he corrected its position.
He told himself that he would have to go out and look in the
mirror to make sure he didn't look freakish. Then he went back
to reading.

*This is from the Feminist Muslim book. It's by a
Muslim woman who's lived in the West. 'In 2013,
when on a trip to India, I had tea with some deso-
late Indian Muslim men and women in Mumbai.
They are a poor, discriminated-against, ill-educated
and powerless minority in a nation increasingly*

dominated by aggressive Hindu nationalists. With all this to contend with, what did they want to talk about the most? (Guess, Jack.) They wanted to know why European and American governments were making Muslims dress like street-walkers and drink alcohol. They were convinced their co-religionists were hapless victims of state-ordered lifestyles.'

Jack didn't know what she was talking about at this point. Agatha didn't say who the author was.

I'm including all this, Jack, because I tried thinking about it. I tried thinking about my 'lifestyle' as oppressive and offensive to Muslims, women as well as men. And I was trying to figure out how I could see things from their perspective. Apparently, people who drink alcohol are 'street-walkers', and this phrase I didn't know before means prostitutes. I drink alcohol, sometimes, and to these people I'm a prostitute. I got angry and then I thought about the section from Disgrace again where Lucy wants to keep her black baby and expects that she will fall in love with it. I don't know if you'll agree, but Miss Lawrence called it a sacrifice. I asked her to explain. She didn't. But what she meant was the pain of being attacked, like Lucy, and having the baby, this was the sacrifice that was necessary.

This was noble. This was her sacrifice for the future of South Africa: having this baby.

And Jack, I read what the Muslim woman had to say about my lifestyle, though I didn't choose it, and I have to tell you that I'm not like Lucy. I'm not prepared. I'm just not ready to make my sacrifice for the future of England. In the future, it probably won't even be called England. But I'm not prepared to make my sacrifice because I don't 'love him', like the book says I have to.

I cannot love him. Because I hate him and Basil and what's happened to me. My mother has paid for it but won't take me to the clinic. She's treating it like a punishment because she has done it so many times before and it is normal to her and not real at all. So could you please answer me if tomorrow you will go with me to the clinic.

She didn't explain herself further, but it was more than enough for Jack to work out what she was talking about. With the weight of what he knew he was being asked to help with, he got up off the toilet seat, and washed his face, and went back out to get drinks with his father. Where was the clinic? He never expected he would have to go to *that* clinic. He didn't even know if Bothelford had one, although according to Agatha, it definitely did. Was there anywhere that didn't have one?

When Jack went through the door outside, the woman from before was gone, and the night air had swept in even though the dark hadn't yet. Jack imagined a black blot forming under the horizon, spreading, and gradually eating away every star in the sky. He sat down at the table with his father, who had gotten himself another drink after finishing his last.

'You were a long time.'

'I got a message from a girl I'm meeting tomorrow,' said Jack.

His father smiled calmly.

'What is it?'

'Is she your girlfriend?'

'No,' said Jack.

'You look disturbed.'

Jack didn't know what to say. He drank his wine.

'She isn't?'

'No!!'

His father leaned in and whispered across the table, 'You haven't gone and gotten a girl pregnant, have you?'

'... No.'

'Phew!' his father laughed. 'Well, why isn't she your girl-friend? Great big lad like you.'

'You're remarkably at ease given the conversation we were just having.'

His father drank.

'Answer the question, Jack.'

'Which?'

'Stop being avoidant. Maybe it isn't my place to ask, but haven't you thought about girls at all? When I was your age—'

'... *I'm not interested in sex.* ...' Jack said, covering his mouth, thinking of the time he got an erection out in the field in front of Agatha.

'You what? What, are you gay or something?'

Jack remembered the dream of Marine Emery playing with his guts and the blue gap in the front of Agatha's mouth.

'I can't explain it well,' said Jack. 'But no, I'm not gay. I just don't want to do things to women.'

His father gave him an odd look. 'Clearly, I shouldn't have asked.'

His father got up and left the table to go and pay the bill. Jack put his hands over his face. His thumbs stuck out over his eyebrows like little horns. He was shading his eyes as they stared directly ahead, wide with a will of their own. His forehead wrinkled. Neither of them talked during the drive back to Bothelford, and Jack could only bring himself to think about meeting Agatha the next day every so often. The stars burned coldly over them.

He had the faint sense before he went to sleep that night in his old bedroom, never having removed the stuffed toys he used to collect from their allocated places on the windowsill, that this reality was haunted by another, different one. Somehow, he knew that things could have been completely different and better than they had turned out. He also knew, as he shut his eyes, that there was absolutely no going back now. The old town was lost with the old world. He wasn't going to meet his girlfriend tomorrow. He didn't have a girlfriend. He watched pornography of women too old for him. Tomorrow, he was going to meet Agatha.

'Tomorrow,' he said. 'I am going to meet Agatha at the abortion clinic.' He wondered whether the rest of his life was going to be just like this.

FOURTEEN

When Jack woke up in the morning, he poured himself a bowl of cereal. He had two cups of coffee. He fixed his glass eye. He took Cipralex and painkillers. He put on a discreet grey jacket. He went into Bothelford. He was going to meet Agatha at 11 a.m. outside St Michael's, and then she was going to walk to the clinic with him. It was a cloudy day. There were occasional shafts of light shooting through the clouds.

Jack walked past the field where he had met Agatha and she had first told him about Basil and Mr Hussein. It was filled with litter. There was no grandmother out collecting it anymore. Jack saw a grey squirrel rush through the side of a crisp packet and felt for a moment tempted to go and collect all the rubbish, partly to escape from seeing Agatha, partly because he was so angered by what he saw. He had heard once about the Old English belief that maggots simply accumulated on bread when the bread was left to grow rotten by itself. The maggots spawned into existence on the food without prior explanation. And so it was with the rubbish. Here it all was, as if summoned according to its own will, like the maggots magically coming out of the bread. He walked on.

When Jack got to the church, he was a minute late, and Agatha was there. Agatha didn't say anything. She was wearing sunglasses, a jumper, and a trench coat. It was quite a warm day, so the clothing looked a little strange. But it only took Jack a second before he realised what its true purpose was. Agatha was dressed in a way that would cover her belly, the very mild, ever so slightly noticeable bump she instinctively held with her left hand inside her jacket. Agatha's knees were asymmetrical, as were her eyes. She was wearing a sunhat, although it wasn't an especially sunny day. Clearly, she wanted to shade her face, hide her shame under a large outfit. When Jack looked at her face, he spotted a crescent bruise under the veil of her fringe. He sighed, then apologised for his lateness. As they walked from St Michael's, and Jack, to distract himself, studied the stained-glass window on the left side of the building featuring Noah's Ark and a great swooping bird that was probably the dove, a Deliveroo driver with a balaclava on the same colour as his face passed them by, and almost fell off of his bike whilst turning the corner. Jack paused and waited for him to sort out his bike, and then the man turned to him and said in a surprisingly high-pitched voice, 'Sorry, buddy.'

Agatha and Jack walked on. Agatha led but didn't want to lead. They passed a sycamore tree—blackbirds were singing in it—and turned through a park. A damaged sign read 'Ascension Play'. Someone had made a daisy crown and discarded it nearby. They passed through the park and into a small, stone, cloistered area with what looked like flats and offices on either side of it. This was the place. It looked like any other building in the world, and yet because Jack knew what it was, it seemed to emanate a kind of subtle brutality. Because Jack had seen documentaries before where animals were slaughtered by Chinese workers in sterile rooms, he imagined sterile rooms. He imagined almost human beings being crushed. And this was the place where it happened.

It had a roof like a Pizza Hut. It looked like a consultancy office. It had glass doors, and if you tightened your gaze, you could see through them and look at some of the people sitting inside. Agatha held his hand tightly in an unfriendly way. He was expected to lead. They had arrived. Jack clicked his knuckles and then pulled Agatha in with him.

The desk of the receptionist was empty. It was purple. The walls were white. There were six people in the waiting room connected to the reception. There was an African woman with two children sitting there, and she did not look pregnant. There was a young white girl browsing a dating app on her phone with smudged eyeliner. There was a fat woman with thick, tarantula-like eyebrows. There was a man in the corner. He was dressed in a black suit. He looked sad.

The chairs were all blue. They were all the same. They were a little bit fuzzy. Their undersides were coated with chewing gum, and occasionally they had scratches on their sides. At the back of the room, opposite the reception desk, there was a kind of free-standing poster that someone had erected. The caption read: 'OUTREACH FOR DIVERSE COMMUNITIES', followed by a series of acronyms. Above all of this was the image of a giant, smiling African man.

There was a bell on the reception desk. Without even concerning herself with Jack, Agatha pressed it. They waited for a minute and a half before an extremely haggard, old woman came out from the office area behind the desk. Jack glanced behind her and saw in the back office an Indian man looking very angry.

'Hello,' said the haggard woman. 'Would you like to book an appointment, or do you have one already?'

'I have one already,' said Agatha.

'Oh, are you Miss Darger?'

'Yes.'

'You're five minutes late, so we might have to push you back.'

'OK,' said Agatha.

'Would you like to go and have a seat over there? I should also say to you that it's our policy that if you want to bring your partner in with you, you can do it.'

'Thank you,' said Agatha. 'That won't be necessary.'

She went over and sat down in the far left corner of the room by herself next to the Outreach poster. Jack studied the room. There were no vending machines. The room was barren. Occasionally, from one of the other rooms, there was the sound of a flickering electric light. There were footsteps. There was the sound of another Indian man talking on the phone somewhere as well as the ongoing racket of the black woman's children playing on their iPads and every so often shrieking at one another. But there was no sign that anything like the procedure that Agatha's mother had booked for her was occurring nearby. It was normal, and it wasn't normal at all.

Jack felt like he was visiting a foreign dictatorship with grey but clean streets, and that he had gone and entered the massive prison system that enabled those streets to remain clean in the first place. This clinic, Jack felt, was the place that ultimately made all the club nights in Bothelford possible, all the accidental products of one-night stands, marriages, and other sexual pairings, followed by more play, more partying, rather than an accounting of sorts. It was interesting in its own way. How would he put it if he had to give a presentation on it in class? The clinic was a secondary contraception in case the pills, condoms, and IUDs failed. The disintegrating sense of fun that the bars and nightclubs bred instead of children relied on the presence of this bland, hidden core. It was filled with unhappy people and, supposedly, a few rooms above, all kinds of surgical tools.

From the other half of the room, Jack heard a clicking noise and realised it was Agatha quietly but aggressively snapping her fingers to get him to come over. Jack walked over to Agatha. He sat down. For some reason, he really needed the toilet, but he didn't want to go.

'Can you come in with me?' Agatha said.

'What? No.'

'Fine,' said Agatha, and didn't speak further. The verdict was final.

Jack started having visions of screaming half-human children. He was thinking about squished brains. He was thinking about himself as a foetus, but aborted.

'How do you feel?' said Jack, slightly stammering.

'I feel like I fucking hate this thing and I want it out and I hate him,' said Agatha.

Jack looked over just above the black kids so that they didn't feel he was being aggressive to them, or leering at them, or intimidating them. The cartoon music from one of the iPads they were using was a remixed version of the song 'The Entertainer'. They chatted, and they made noises, and they did not speak English. Their mother was absolutely unbothered.

The man in the corner was on his phone now as well. He was rapidly moving his thumbs and fingers in different directions, and it seemed like he was messaging multiple people at once. He had grey hair. He had a long nose. He had thick black eyebrows. Jack imagined that this was somebody's father. He couldn't tell if he was the father of the girl in the operating theatre or the father of the baby inside of her. Jack only assumed there was one operating theatre and one girl. He also assumed, for his own sanity, that Agatha had not been here many times before.

She looked ill at ease enough for him to assume that this was her first time. But maybe that was just the situation she had found herself in. There was no ease here, nothing at all like that.

Jack decided that he was going to stand up and wander a little around the room. He couldn't sit still, nor did he want to. How far away was the operating theatre? He still imagined just the one. How far away was the girl who must be in there right now? As he moved from one part of the waiting room to the other, feeling almost drunk, the distance that he,

Jack Grundon, was from the operating theatre in some other part of the building became extremely important to him. On the left side of the waiting room, was he eleven metres away? On the right side of the waiting room, was he twelve metres away? Was he fourteen metres or fifteen metres? Was he nine or was he ten? The difference between eleven metres and twelve metres frightened him, that proximity to births receiving death.

'Sit *down*,' said Agatha. She was addressing him like a naughty little boy.

He sat down. He looked at her belly, the bump. Agatha exhaled, and he looked away.

Jack imagined what this child of Agatha and Basil's would have been like, that is, if Basil were the father. In his head, Jack saw the smiling face of a darkly complexioned boy with his father's eyes playing with toy trucks next to a mother with a dead-eyed stare and a knife in her hands. It didn't really work. He didn't want to imagine Agatha cutting the baby's head off with the knife, but he already had.

Was that what she was doing? Was that what Basil and the gang had forced upon her, were forcing on Jessie Waters, had forced already on hundreds and maybe thousands of others? Jack imagined three women, all of them young, all of them ter-rified in front of giant mechanical centipedes that threatened to enter them. He couldn't think of it. And yet he had thought of it. Did he think of robot centipedes because he didn't know what abortionist surgical tools looked like? He didn't want to know what they looked like. But this was no better.

His imagination deepened, and he dropped down into it as into a well. He saw himself strolling through a dark, desolated place that was and was not where he belonged. There was no sun. He came to the central square. He thought of the chimera, now with the body of a centipede, grinning down at him atop a war memorial absolutely drenched in urine. All the English names were replaced with melting graffiti in Urdu and Arabic. He couldn't but imagine it somehow. He had to imagine it. He imagined the chimera's cartoonish face with the wide grinning mouth of Officer Fahir speaking to him, to him, Mad Jack, in front of these three writhing forms, these terrified innocents about to be entered by the centipedes. The Chimera of Rape said to him: 'THIS IS WHAT THEY LET US DO TO YOU.' Jack was trembling.

Agatha could see that Jack was trembling. Whatever he was thinking about was making him tremble. Agatha also started trembling.

Jack felt like he was on camera, being laughed at by someone. He trembled. He was sick in the head to think like this.

There was the sound of a metal bin jolting on its side in the other room. Agatha held Jack's hand. The haggard lady from before came out.

'You can come in now,' she said to Agatha.

'Others have waited longer,' said Agatha.

'Come in now.'

Agatha nodded, looked at Jack with the widest eyes he had ever seen on a woman, and then she followed the old woman into the other room. Jack couldn't but imagine the chimera laughing at him with its six tongues. There was only deterioration. There was only excess. He wanted to spit into his own face like it was a dirty sewer opening. Whatever he was feeling was what the father over in the corner was feeling. He grabbed the wastepaper bin by the Outreach poster and vomited his cereal up from that morning. She was gone. Agatha was getting an abortion.

A minute passed that felt like an eternity. What was beginning to happen in there, in that secret room now?

Thirty seconds more passed. How long did he have to wait? How many more minutes? He was getting visions of the centipedes, and then he was sick again. 'Are they on the kid's fucking brain? Are they in her yet?' he asked himself. He hit himself in the face. He breathed.

'Fuck,' he said. 'Fuck. Fuck. Fuck.'

He wanted to kill Basil and all the gang members, and he wanted to kill Agatha for making him come here, and he wanted to kill himself. He imagined himself being cut up by chainsaws, and the chimera was still laughing. He couldn't take it. He took his Cipralex. He couldn't take it. He wanted to start punching holes in the walls. He imagined Agatha as a happy mother with a little girl who looked just like her, and he started sobbing. He was not meant to live in this world, right here, right now, but that one, the one where that was possible. And this was even truer of Agatha. She was meant to live there, not here.

What had she done to deserve this, all this? This wasn't a moral universe; Jack had long known that. But how could it be this evil? He glanced at the smiling African face on the Out-reach poster, and it seemed to laugh at him with the voice of the chimera. They were the same after all. The chimera, as it had told him in a dream many years before, was Bothelford's King of Kings. It was everywhere. It ruled. It normalised things.

What had happened to Agatha was now just the kind of thing that happened in the United Kingdom. The curtains of the operating theatre closed.

FIFTEEN

It was a half an hour wait until Agatha came out. In that time, the father in the corner of the room had also started weeping. He exchanged glances with Jack in commiseration but nothing more. The black woman's children played on their iPads, and one of them hit the other. The young white girl used a tissue to wipe the eyeliner on her face when she was taking a selfie to use on the dating app. The fat woman breathed in quiet rumbles.

All the while, Jack had heard nothing but imaginary laughter. His strength had collapsed. He no longer hit himself in the face. He just saw fragmented baby heads wherever he looked. He had no idea how long the procedure was meant to take, and he dared not look it up on his phone. He realised as soon as Agatha came out that he had no idea how many weeks or months pregnant she had been. When he saw her, he decided not to ask. He looked at her. He felt no relief. He wanted to get out.

Agatha's eyes were sparkling, wide. Her mouth looked ruffled and blackened and thinner somehow. It was the mouth of a puppet that had had all the stuffing taken out of its head. She was walking in a jittery way. All her fingers were stretched out as she went to the reception desk. There was also an energy in her eyes that couldn't be found in any other area of her body, a liveliness, even, in being disburdened. She signed off on a series of forms in addition to the ones she had presumably signed in the other room. She didn't ask for Jack's hand. She was clearly furious that he hadn't gone in with her. She exited by herself, and Jack helplessly followed. Her pace was rapid. She wasn't speaking. Her long blonde hair flopped behind her like a dead weight. Jack bit his nails, as had become his habit.

He got up, breathed the air of the clinic hopefully for the last time ever, and started walking behind her outside. When they passed a homeless man in the street who told Agatha, 'Can you *please* take me to the credit card machine, love?' she scowled and said to Jack, 'Deal with this.'

He spoke to the man. She continued in the other direction. She was headed towards a café, near St Michael's, with a big wooden swan carved above the main window, which was open on that day because of the warmth. Jack stopped talking to the man and caught up with her.

'I'm sorry I wasn't there,' said Jack.

'You're glad you weren't there. I'd be glad if I weren't there. But I was there.'

She walked on into the café and went past the oak tables and a set of old men drinking coffee and soda, and she asked the Indian woman at the till if the vodka bottle behind the bar was a decoration or if it was for sale.

'Is no for sale that one. But we can do other.'

'Get me it,' said Agatha. 'He will pay for it.'

Jack had just entered. He heard this. He pulled out his credit card. He was living on an allowance his father had given him out of pity after his run-in with the police. The Indian woman went and got shot glasses.

'No,' said Agatha, impulsively. 'Can we have two empty glasses? For water.'

The Indian woman nodded and pulled out two tall glasses with hexagonal bases from behind the counter. Jack paid and took the bottle of vodka. Agatha took the glasses. They went and sat in the right corner of the café by the bathroom.

Jack poured Agatha's glass. He said he didn't want one. He set the bottle down. Then Agatha poured Jack's glass for him regardless. Her seat was uncomfortable. She stood up to adjust her coat, and a black boy and his friend came out of the toilet and slapped her on the backside. They ran off cackling out of the café as the Indian woman shook her head.

'Meat,' said Agatha. 'I am meat. Meat.' She lifted the glass with her little wrist and drank.

Jack drank. He could feel his stomach lining react. He drank.

'I wanted to win against the fucking doctors, Jack. Then, at the last minute, when they had it out, I told them that they had to keep it safe. Keep it safe!'

She drank. Jack drank.

'I'm not going to make it through the whole bottle,' Jack said.

'I am going to make it through the whole bottle,' Agatha said. 'So either fucking sit here and drink it with me or fuck off home. I have a hole in my heart.'

Jack poured his glass full of vodka. He drank three-quarters of it. It burned. He started spluttering.

'Fucking men,' said Agatha. '*Fucking* men.'

'Which men?'

'You know what I'm talking about. You know who I'm talking about. We always mean the same people when we say *men*.'

Jack drank the remaining quarter glass. The café had a TV playing sports in the area by the old men drinking coffee. He couldn't tell if it was football or rugby. The old men were getting quite animated in their discussion about it. They really cared about the men playing with the ball. Agatha drank three-quarters of her own glass and then refilled it to the top so that she could begin drinking again. The Indian woman was giving her a funny look from behind the counter.

'Let's get drunk tonight,' said Agatha. 'Then walk me home.'

'OK,' said Jack.

'Give me your entire tube of Cipralex.'

Jack found it in his jacket and gave it to her.

'We'll take these later.'

'I'm not taking any.'

'Drink up.'

He did. Agatha poured him another.

'What do you want to do with your life?' she said.

'That's a bit sudden.'

'Mmmmmn.'

As Jack didn't answer, Agatha started drinking and going on Instagram on her phone. She spun the camera around and

showed Jack a clip that automatically came up. It was an adver-
tisement for stab-proof vests and showed Afghan schoolchildren wearing balaclavas outside a Morrison's in Nottingham
with '#UKVESTPLUG' and '#PROTECTYOURCHEST'
emblazoned over the screen. She didn't have to look for anything in particular. The algorithm merely showed her what
was on her mind, which was apparently the accumulating mass
of violent young foreigners. One day soon, that would be the
whole country, Jack thought. One day soon, that would be the
entirety of Europe. Agatha drank. A minute of silence passed.

'... That day I first met you out on the field by the school,' said
Jack, nervously. 'you were wearing a Pentagram or something.'

'Yeah. *Not now*,' Agatha said in a tiny voice.

'Why wear it in the first place?' Jack asked. He was trying to
fill in the vacuum of just sitting there with her, the void behind
it all. He was, for some reason, conscious that her pupils had
holes in them, and so did his own. That's what pupils were,
after all, and yet he felt the openings and how he was looking
through them at her.

'I like emo music, so that's why I wore it,' said Agatha, quickly.
'Deafheaven, maybe, I guess. But—do you know "Tek It", like
the song "Tek It"? It's by this duo ... Ka-Fune, or some shit.
There's a shoegaze version. *Do you know Hayley Williams?*'

'No.'

'Course you wouldn't ... Bro, "Tek It" 's good. Like—'

She rolled her eyes back and started shaking a little bit,
tuned into the memory of snare drums and mumbled: '*And
how much can I be expected to tol-er-ate? Oo—*'

'What's that?'

'—*We star-ted off in such a nice place ... we were talk-in' the same lan-gu-age ...* You're taking the piss, Jack, *interrupting ...* Forget where I was now. Anyway.'

Agatha drank her entire glass and refilled her entire glass.

'AAH!' she said, and clapped.

'What!?' said Jack.

'I stopped wearing it,' she said, laughing. 'The pin, because it gave me ... made me feel sick. Or something. Plus, like, I was hanging out with Basil, and I thought that I'd go and get all dark and frighten him—you know Muslims are scared of spells, or meant to be—and I put it on and I made some noises, and the piece of shit just pinched his nose and cackled. Ugggghhh—'

Jack drank half of his glass and refilled half of his glass.

'There's this show I like,' said Agatha. 'Called *The Amazing Digital Circus*; it's on YouTube. You can watch it—'

Jack drank a little bit more, and Agatha giggled in a high octave; Jack had to admit she had an extremely good singing voice. He remembered his distant relative, the singer Theresa.

'Hey—have you heard of Theresa—'

'—It's about this girl who gets sucked into her computer and wakes up, and she's a clown-person, and she has to do all these *like* challenges, and it sucks, but she also doesn't need to ever eat or sleep, so that's all right, and sometimes I like thinking about being her. Dye my hair. Dress up for Halloween. Paint my skin white. And when is Halloween? Like, no, Jack, no *interrupting* me ...' she sniggered.

Jack wanted to get some water, but Agatha called him a 'bitch bo-*i*', and that was that. She and Jack drank for as long as it took her to finish muttering about the clown girl stuck in another world and how this reminded her of herself and how she couldn't get back either to the life she had once had or ... to her little black cat whom she missed. Then when she nearly started crying again and before Jack could get her to leave with him, Agatha herself changed the subject, muttering through a drunken haze deeper and darker, throbbingly.

'Whatdoyouwannadowhenyougrowup.'

'A binman,' said Jack.

'Why?'

'When I'm going somewhere, I instinctively pick up empty juice cartons and glass bottles and throw them away. I've cut my hands before doing it; I do it all the same. If I could do it for pay, I'd do it every day.'

'Wouldyoufightthosewholikedroppedit?'

'I'd be a binman plus crime fighter. Baton in one hand, rubbish bag in another.'

'Whathappenedtoyoureyethough ...'

Jack realised that she must have been so absorbed by the prospect of the visit to the clinic that she hadn't truly taken notice of his appearance until now.

Jack sighed. He brushed hair from over the scars on his skull. He fiddled with his glass eye.

'I was hit in the head with a hammer in the police station.'

'Ow,' said Agatha. She drank a little and shook her head three times.

'I have a glass eye. Look.'

She leaned in. 'Wow. Real.'

'What about you?'

'What?' said Agatha.

Jack drank.

'What do you want to do after A Levels? For your future?'

'A princess,' she said. 'When I was growing up, I wanted to be a princess.'

Jack paused. He didn't know if he should continue, but then he did.

'Well ...' he said. 'What about now?'

'I want to be a princess,' said Agatha. 'Anything is possible. Anything is possible.'

SIXTEEN

As Jack lay hungover in his bedroom the next morning, he began to recall fragments of what had happened the night before.

Their conversation had descended into mumbles, and they had been made to leave the café after Agatha had gotten up to go to the bathroom and smashed her glass by mistake. The walk back to hers had been quick. The leering eyes of dark faces outside of bars had passed over Agatha. Some women had looked at Jack, recognising him from the internet, from the stories, and reels, and videos that had been made about him with this same girl. One of them had strode up to Jack, as confident as anything, wielding her camera. But Agatha had brushed her away. Past these bulging crowds, they had made their way back to St Michael's and opposite it towards where Agatha lived. White bodies had accumulated at one end of the road, blacks at the other. White women and black men had met in the middle, the same area where some mixed-race men and women could have been seen. The groups had been organised according to absolute principles that one half of their membership weren't permitted to know or understand. Jack and Agatha had lurched down a road.

And there was the house. In the night, the house looked white and old. But the door had been ultra-modern, futurist even. It looked like a hard piece of stone with no carvings on it of any kind, no decorations. It was an old house with a slab instead of a door and a door handle with a fake, red ruby embedded in it. The door couldn't have belonged to the original house. Jack had wondered whether it was purchased using the money that Agatha's father left behind. There was a darkened window near the door, and Jack had looked through it and seen a large smoky room with two sinks and what appeared to be a custom-made, electric light that said *Barbiecore*.

It was at this point that Jack's memory grew foggy. The door had opened, firstly just a little bit. And then it seemed to glitch into a kind of wound or mouth in the side of Agatha's house. A figure had emerged with porcelain skin and very black hair. Jack couldn't recall her walking. She had levitated over like a broken statue recovered from a tomb using wires. The figure had said something, maybe two things. He couldn't recall either. Agatha had entered the mouth with that figure, that lure. The door had sealed again.

Jack had wandered home. He had stood briefly outside a pub and wondered if he should buy something. There were some South African men standing around outside smoking. He recalled how, from one of the upper rooms, a glass bottle had landed about two feet away from his head. The South African men had gotten angry and went first to the staff to complain and then upstairs. There was the sound of rustling and shouting. But by then, Jack had gone.

He had knocked on the door of his mother's house. His mother had been there. She had grown fatter. She had grown older. Her eyes had big bags under them. She frequently cried by herself because she was going through the menopause, the beginning of it, and Jack felt guilty for accelerating the process by stressing her out, or that's what he believed had occurred. Almost instantaneously, he had gone upstairs and then to sleep. He hadn't managed to take off his clothes. He had dreamt of the colour red, just red, in memory.

When he got up in the morning, there was the faint smell of vomit on his shirt sleeves. But he was only properly awakened by the sound of his father pressing the doorbell. That day, for the first time, his father was going to take him to the gym. But Jack had totally forgotten about it. And so the door was pushed down, the mess of Jack's room was revealed, and his father shouted at him for the first time in years. Jack went to the bathroom and drank a litre and a half of water. Then he drank just enough coffee so that it wouldn't dry him out to the point of unconsciousness. He drank another half-litre of water. He washed. Not yet, his mind said. He drained the fluid out of his eye socket and placed his glass eye in. He remembered Mrs Darger, that levitating statue. He dressed in his gym kit and vomited into the sink and lay himself down in bed. There was some shouting. There was some vomit in front of him. What could be done? Involuntarily, he fell half asleep and then woke up again after his father had said he was heading back down the stairs and out of the house. Jack saw him as he groaned and passed from sight: a pale grey head on grey shoulders sinking. He was gone. That was a day ruined, Jack thought.

Jack twisted in his bed to regard his hot, charged phone. The screen smelled. He would change the subject. His father: what did he have to say about his father? The man had secured a livelihood without maintaining a marriage; in any other historical context but the modern one, Jack wondered, would it have been conceivable that his life was something other than a failure, a shame? And now that shame had deepened because of Jack, his actions, and because John Grundon, his father, was no longer himself anymore but the one responsible for raising him: Mad Jack, the undesirable lunatic who had squandered, all in one go, his serious chance of getting into a good university and due to striking Basil, the reputation of his entire family. Even if all the accusations of his assault on Agatha were cleared up, that stain would linger. 'Funny how everyone pretends that honour doesn't exist,' Jack thought to himself, 'but as soon as you embarrass yourself in the wrong way—not by molesting a girl, but by acting against the one inconveniently responsible—suddenly it's the Victorian Age again ...' (He browsed on his phone.) '... Except Victoria, the mother of all colonists, will have her statues thrown into the pit soon enough. And when they're all gone, they'll come for you.' He couldn't think about Agatha.

Jack turned and groaned slightly and rolled over on his back, and wondered what he was going to look up. In Islam, he had researched, the alcohol prohibition seemed to be there in

order to prevent a perhaps naturally more aggressive Arab peas-
antry from committing all kinds of additional sins, above all,
the sexual ones. Fair enough: he neither despised the religion,
nor could he deny the significance of the Prophet to so many.
It was just alien, and he wouldn't ever understand it because
it wasn't for him or for his country. Yet, perhaps, hungover—
miserably panting over his sweat-dampened pillow—Jack for
once understood the attitude to drinking of his silent neighbour Fatima. Because, hungover, Jack was overstimulated, and
the alcohol spun around inside him and made him consider
doing things he wouldn't usually.

He searched the internet for a Mrs Alice Darger. He found
her CV—an optician's receptionist—and then more palat-
able images of her than Basil had once shown him. She had
a chalk-white face in every image and eyelashes that curved
so deeply into her eyes that her eyes looked black. She had
had numerous surgeries, and she was tattooed just enough to
achieve an alluring contrast between the vulgarity of the words
scrawled over her and her natural pallor: 'bad bitch', 'Wan-
nabeMILF', and what appeared to be a meaningless arabesque.

The Muslims clearly liked her because she was white and
played up being white, even deliberately coming across as a
bratty, nagging caricature of all the irritating white English
women they had encountered in the school system, in their
office jobs, and outside their restaurants and kebab vans in the
night, and that meant that breaking her in would feel all the
better. Jack estimated all this and felt alien in his own head
as he did so, and yet he still clicked on one of her short teaser

clips and watched the first thirty seconds of a video of her imitating a secondary schoolteacher with red marks on her throat. Jack wondered if one of his former classmates, maybe Jamal, had even requested this video. The character was too precise not to have been based on a real person: the bitter way she read Maths grades aloud, the odd precision of 'Anna-Marie Garnett', the character's name. It was reasonable to assume that this was some white woman an audience member had hated, which meant that Alice Darger's job, if it wasn't simply sexual slavery, was partly to imitate white women her audience despised and wanted to vengefully fuck. Jack closed the video when he saw blonde hair in the background in the mirror.

'Was Agatha … no!' he said to himself; he held his head in his hands; she had been filming her Mum.

The skin on Jack's head was hot, hotter than it felt inside his head, if that were even possible to know. He hadn't gone so far as to join Alice Darger's audience by actually masturbating to what he saw in front of him, but he had watched it, the opening at least. He imagined a crowd of bearded figures in a cinema, proclaiming, 'Welcome, Jack! Welcome, Jack!' The room transformed into the old Georgian theatre he used to see the pantomime at with his parents. In one opera box, sitting with a big cigar was Abdul Hussein and his brother, and in another was the Ali that Basil had mentioned screaming, '… Bid'ah!'. Jack imagined them smiling and sneering at him for supposing himself to be above enjoying Mrs Darger and her daughter. Well, now he was involved, their friend, their fellow consumer, they offered him peanuts and chips before

the lifting, grey stage curtains behind which something suffered that he was too much of a coward to lay his eyes on. Jack
groaned. He put his pillow over his face and removed it when
he found it hard to breathe. He coughed a little and thought
about pacing the room.

'So evil,' he said, lowly. 'What am I supposed to call it? Evil.
It is evil.'

What he didn't say aloud, but felt shiver through his head
against his own will, was the new fact that he had just realised:
that he too was evil. He was evil and had been made to participate in evil in order to prevent him from fighting it. Jack
didn't feel this to be an exaggeration, and he knew—he just
knew—on some level that this was a tactic of the chimera. For,
in another age, he could have banded together with friends
and reported Basil and Hussein and even Fahir, and the whole
village would have joined him in combat, supplied him with
arms, even as they took him lovingly into their own. Even in
the nineteen-seventies, in a mass society where populations of
millions could be spread and shifted at the will of insane governments across the West, he could have resisted or attempted
to resist the gangs, what they did, what they had already
done. But today? Today, he, as a citizen of the United Kingdom's flourishing, multicultural democracy, had a device in
his pocket that his own parents had bought him when he was
fourteen that enabled him to watch one of the victims being
humiliated and tortured whenever it pleased him. If he were
interested in the fate of a particular girl, Jack knew he could
look her up, and have his tastes cultivated to be more like the

predators he had told himself he wanted to bring to justice. It
was evil, and he was part of the evil. In order to destroy it, he
would have to destroy part of himself, or simply himself. He
couldn't think about Agatha.

As Jack looked over the hot phone screen and shut the power
off and he saw his own darting, predatory eyes reflected in the
black glass, he began to understand the meaning of the phone
and what it really was. He went to the bathroom and poured
himself a water. He drank and sat; his pulse was irritated and
irregular, but his mind was lucid. Sane, on the verge of being
sober again, he realised an aspect of life in which he had been
insane for almost all of it. What did his phone do? The phone
enabled him to watch thirty seconds of Alice Darger, and that
option, that humiliation would now always be available for
him to 'enjoy'—no matter the circumstances. This possibility
had always existed since he had been given his phone, and so
did watching pornography, in general, which was more unreal,
strange, and terrifying than anything his entire ancestral line
had ever been exposed to in their youth. Therefore, Jack concluded, the phone was a porn device with additional features
decorating and disguising this central fact.

And so, Jack worked out, the truth was that Jamal's parents
had gotten Jamal a porn device and so had Muhammad Akbar's,
and Agatha had a porn device also and so did so many of the
children Jack knew as a boy in his online classes during the
pandemic that the effects on their entire generation were too
great to be encompassed by any one analysis. Certainly, yes, for
some, childhood would have been nothing less than violent

pornography interspersed with execution videos, and little else but that. Once, in Miss Lawrence's class, a boy named Ethan had shown him Afghans falling to their deaths from the side of a US aircraft. But that was nothing: he must have been fifteen or sixteen, and at that time, a challenge called Run the Gauntlet was popular with the boys. The goal was to watch twenty videos that grew increasingly more difficult to watch. Jack hadn't seen any, but he had heard the boys speak about them to each other: a woman drowning in a bathtub, a baby being run over by a train. If they were fourteen and fifteen and they had seen those videos, then someone in the school would have seen them at six or seven, five or four, from the start. A little brother, a girl.

But if violence was one thing, then sex was another. Jack dreaded to think what had been shown to Agatha by her own mother to brainwash her into what she was becoming. Such imagery was weaponry. Wherever it was shown, there was always either a motivation to attack or evidence of the state's, the rulers' negligence. Porn indoctrinated young Englishmen with shame at the same time as it incentivised foreigners to come and replicate the sex acts they had seen performed on white women over the internet. Jack didn't want to know that the disproportionate majority of porn actresses were white, and yet, of course, he did by now.

Jack turned over in his bed and stopped thinking about porn. He said to himself loudly, 'What am I going to do today?' before shifting his eyes from one wall to another, and grinding his teeth until he heard a faint and slightly concerning snap. He didn't know what the sound was. He checked his teeth in the mirror of his phone screen. They looked fine. When he returned to his bedroom and saw his stained, blue cushion with sweat on it and the disordered, twisted blanket under which he had slept, with the design of an incubus squatting dead in the middle of it, he noticed there was now a mysterious, brown twig on the bed. The twig was exactly where his back would have been when he was sleeping. Perhaps he had been so drunk when he'd gotten to bed that he simply hadn't felt it. But, if he was honest, Jack didn't know why it was there. It had a brown, bulbous head and three arms sticking out of it, two of them roughly at the equivalent of the twig's shoulder level. It looked very much like a doll, and Jack was thinking of going and showing it to his parents before he realised neither of them would ever be in the mood to appreciate it. Instead, he decided to remove it from his bed and leave it out the front, past the drive, in case someone else found it amusing enough to take home. He didn't think about Agatha.

Jack told himself that leaving the twig outside would be a neighbourly thing to do as well as a distracting thing to do. It was moronic, but whatever. Jack got dressed and went down the stairs. At this point, he realised he could probably have gone to the gym in the first place and promised himself that next time he would have to go no matter the circumstances. When he put his socks on, Jack noticed the healing scars around his ankle where Basil had stabbed him, the scab that looked like a recently formed mountain range, a border. He put on his shoes. He left through the front door and didn't think about Agatha for as long as he could.

SEVENTEEN

'So, what am I going to do today?' Jack said to himself, walking out of the house. He decided to think about the government, the state—how his behaviour had effectively sealed him off from the elite, from real power, from work, and could similarly immiserate his parents in the long run: kicking Basil in the genitals. But when he almost thought about Agatha again, he decided to think about the state exclusively from then on, and this time, its connection to the internet. Jack would add more details in order to keep the spectre of the girl away, seal out her memory with irrelevance. What of the internet? In the nineteen-eighties, Fauna Williams wouldn't have been able to record Basil Alawi, secretly, without the agreement of some TV organiser. And if that man hadn't wanted the story of Agatha's group molestation on the news, then it wouldn't have been put on. Maybe the internet, for all that Jack had just railed against internet pornography, had also made Fauna's recording possible in the first place. In other words, it had allowed information to escape from the control of the class of managers who ran the TV and the state, and because of that, it would have to be gotten rid of, Jack predicted, maybe the whole internet, within the next ten years. (Agatha was half-deleted from Jack's head.)

The internet models of China and Russia would be almost identical to what was coming to the West, Jack considered, only the new Western internet would censor itself to suppress 'misinformation', rather than to quash dissent—though, of course, they were the same exact thing. That seemed true. Fauna's information-based activism was simply too good at interfering with the story about reality that such managers wanted to tell, Jack told himself. And so, the internet had to be deconstructed and annihilated, and it had already largely disappeared. For, in his early youth, Jack remembered hundreds of digital worlds, places online where thousands of people would pretend to be characters, roleplay, wander through polygonal graveyards under a camera angled down as if from Paradise. But what was left of all that now? There were just four or five real platforms of significance now, and that was it. The vanishing would continue. Jack decided that this would generally be a good thing because the end of the internet would force him to act in the real world and acquire friends he could rely on, as opposed to requiring Fauna's vacuous, unreal audience to accomplish anything.

Jack went through all these different thoughts in his head about the significance of returning to reality and the end of the internet, and as he walked out down the lawn and past the gate, he saw, suddenly, that there was rubbish all the way up and down his street, the street he had grown up on, and more of it than he had ever seen there before. So this was the real world.

'Leave aside the internet, your thoughts,' Jack told himself. 'and gaze into it.' Jack smelled the dead rat crushed up amongst glass bottles before he saw it, and then he saw that there were three large piles, just below the size where they might prevent cars from moving, spilling out from the pavement and assorted cans, pizza boxes, rice packets, loo rolls, broken plates and bent kitchenware, toys with green stains on them, and rotten cabbages and beans displaced in a long trail that finished with the biggest pile of all. Jack looked at the trail on the road outside his house with eyes agog and was immediately reminded of the diagram of a spermatozoid.

Why was it all just there?

Piles and piles and piles, box after box, strewn meats and vegetables, wrappers.

A few potential answers came to Jack as he stared, and walked, and saw nobody else on the street go by. Given that he had grown understandably paranoid concerning the fact that gang members with representation in the police knew who he was, he instinctively assumed that the scene out on the street where he lived was designed to intimidate him, let him know that they knew where his mother stayed. But did they really care that much about him, the gang? Did they really see him as such a potential threat that this low-grade, piffling harassment was necessary? If they wanted to send him a message, wouldn't it have been better to opt for something unmistakable, like the severed horse or cat head from a mafia film? A signal like this one, if it was a signal, rubbish everywhere, was ineffective due to the fact that it was entirely disguised by the process most simply referred to as the Decline of the West that was already underway. For binmen were on strike in their part of England.

'Bro, why did the kafir not get the message, bro?' Jack imagined one gang member saying.

'It's the Decline of the West, innit, bro?' said another. 'Itz in the wey.'

That was Jack's first answer: moronic gang intimidation. His second one was that he himself had been so alienated from his home and from his own street that he hadn't noticed the changes as they gradually occurred and that his parents, busy with the nightmare of agitating for a better life for their criminal son, had neglected to pick the litter up from the road. Yes, instantly, Jack knew the second answer was the correct one, and in his heart, he felt both the pain of knowing that he had little to no connection with the land that was his inheritance and the pride and joy of having such parents. For the reason why their home had never looked like the dump it had so rapidly become was exclusively, obviously due to the influence of John Grundon and Mary Phillips, who were divorced and yet still did their best for him. When he was twelve, he had glanced at them working together to pluck the bodies of badgers from the side of the road and decorate the front of the lane with honesty boxes and flowers, as he had sat for ages at a screen and meditated on the issues of fate and destiny, of himself and the fate of the West.

Well, here was the West! It was dirty and grey and hideous, and strewn with bent cutlery, and empty packages, and mangoes thrown out and half-consumed by people who did not care for nature or for public cleanliness. The West? On this street, there was no 'West', but for his parents. He had assumed that there was, or once had been, but there hadn't been—not before they and their ilk came, and they were among the first, unlike such petulant newcomers as dropped their garbage. There had been chaos, and they had come, even after being divorced, not simply to try their best to raise him, but to hammer such disorder into form in the world in general. It was their land, and they were entitled to it to the same extent that they had maintained it, as well as its simply being their birth-right. This tender care for the land, Jack had scoffed at more than once in his early youth. He had even said to himself more recently that Bothelford couldn't be saved, that the demo-graphic trends were too bad, that it wouldn't be worth saving. And yet the difference between the street then and now was night and day. He had spoken of evil. Here was the material difference between evil and good.

Jack went into the house, got the bin bags out, and cut himself accidentally on a glass bottle when he reached for it. He threw the bottle down into one of the bags. Now, he had decided what he was going to do that day. He followed the trail with the bags and filled one almost exclusively with big rice packets, then knotted it as best as he could in his untrained way. He dissected the big pile of rubbish with bits of wood sticking out of it, with broken chair legs, and snapped them down to a more manageable size. He diminished the pile and emptied its contents into three different bags. The crushed body of the dove he found within it he decided he would bury later because he liked doves. The strange twig he had found in his bed that morning he rested on a fence nearby, and thought of it as his sentinel, his overseer.

Jack didn't suck the blood from his hands as it flowed but continued packing. After the first pile had been emptied into four bags, he went in and washed his hands clean, and then he put gloves on. He went to the second and then the third, and replicated the procedure over the course of three hours, and gradually felt the soreness in his liver alleviate as he recovered from last night's alcohol.

He tore a bag going through the glass parts of the trail, and found himself thinking of what would happen if a child on the street ended up tripping and falling on the glass. 'This was all completely necessary,' he thought. He went inside and got the bag that he confirmed to be for glass, and went out and transferred one bag into another. Subsequently, he managed to fit all the glass into one bag and realised he had to tie the knot in a specific way that would enable him to lift the bag without accidentally gripping it and cutting himself. He searched the internet on his phone and found a method proposed by a Texan handyman, tried it, and managed to secure a strong enough knot that he wouldn't have to rely on picking up the bag by gripping the entire top in order to transport it. Satisfied with this method, he then untied the knots on all his other plastic bags and retied them in the style that the American had taught him. He then piled the bags in a line, going from smallest to largest, and within only half an hour managed to decimate the obnoxious tail of the spermatozoid that had so offended and confused him when he first saw it. He finished at around five o'clock, without having eaten for the whole day. The days were starting to shorten, and the sun was lower than usual. And so, he finished as the day did.

Jack looked over the street and what he had accomplished in the evening sun. His mother was out until seven to see a friend of hers. His father was God knew where. What was the right word for what he had done to the street? He had *restored* it. He had restored, with only his own efforts, however unskilfully, his home to how it used to look in his childhood on many an unimportant, boring night. And for almost half a minute, he wasn't trying to distract himself from the abortion or the rape of Agatha Darger. He knew what had happened, but he was tending to the land, his land, and this was now ever so slightly less of a place where either of those sorts of things could happen! Ridiculous as it might have been to think, he sincerely believed that he had reduced the amount of evil in the area and weakened the influence of those who occupied his home. He felt that he had made it just a bit less like hell, and that he had brought a sliver of Bothelford back. His back was sore, his arms ached with the effort of his work, and he remembered the motto above the Two Brewers: *By the sweat of thy brow shalt thou earn thy bread.*

He asked himself before the headlamps of a passing car, 'What if I did this every three weeks? Or, *no*, what if I did this and then later this week I decided to plant a few flowers? What would really prevent me from going out and buying some poppy seeds, some lilies, and planting them on the grass verges and in the alleys? Maybe I would need planning permission. But there's a chance I could do it without anyone noticing. Then it would rain, and they would grow. And what if I worked with my parents? What if I wanted to clean the road itself with a specialised hose, and built a birdhouse, and left seeds there daily, and I befriended the birds? What if, after everyone forgets about my damaged reputation and moves on to the next ridiculous person, I get a job as a plumber or a binman? Aren't they supposed to make a lot of money doing the work no one else is bothered to do? Why not?––And if I can't, well, why can't I keep going to the pub, join a sports team, get a hobby, meet some local lads? Whoever cares about university grades is going to want to get rid of me anyway. So why, if I worked with my parents, and then I made some friends who were interested, couldn't I set up a service across town? What if we cleaned it all up together, regularly, out of love for the place? Wouldn't that make everyone happier? What if we were paid to do the cleaning and then we set up some art classes with the extra cash, or what if—after everything we would have already done—we got some of our friends in the police or on the local council? Wouldn't that change everything?'

As the car passed, a big four-by-four, Jack noticed what looked like Fatima in the back passenger seat amongst her numberless children. He turned and let his gaze follow it as six crushed Diet Coke cans fell out onto the street from the left window on its side.

EIGHTEEN

And then Jack didn't want to be at the house when his parents returned. It was too much, just being there now. He had seen too much, felt too much. He felt like smoking a cigarette, although he had never had one. Maybe that would be the next thing. He would go down into Bothelford to some late-night off-licence and buy himself his first packet of Rothmans Gold or whatever he could afford. That sounded like a plan. As for the bags of rubbish, rubble, glass, he would leave them there by the side of the road for his mother to find. Perhaps she would attribute the labour that had gone into clearing up the street to Jack's father and thank him for it later. Jack wondered to himself whether this was going to be his last gift to the deteriorated remains of their marriage. He imagined their union personified, a strange enmeshment of young man and girl, and himself setting upon its head a plastic wreath. He felt awful for disappointing his father with his drunkenness that morning. It was too bad that this was the end. Why, so universal, was there this sense of the end?

Jack went back inside the house and put on a light black jacket in the kitchen. It was his father's, but he wore it nowadays. He took the key on the side, set the burglar alarm with the familiar passcode (his own date of birth), and locked the door behind him. It was colder now, colder out. He zipped up his coat but found that the zip jammed in the wire two-thirds up. Intuition guided him, and as he went down the road on his left, turning around the tarmac of the basketball court, and then right, then down the hill, sloping through cement and red brick ways under angular, buzzing lamps, he didn't know if he was headed anywhere in particular or simply off the edge of a river bridge. The end.

What was he feeling? The urge to leave, leave here, Bothelford, wasn't even prompted by the act of littering he had just seen. It was harder to explain than that. He had to put his hands in his jacket as they shivered, and he regretted not bringing gloves with him, the leather ones he had seen on the kitchen side, also his father's. He felt a deep need to escape his home because it felt inappropriate that he could live where he always had and be as he was—act, at least, like he used to—when he had, self-evidently, utterly, and inoperably, changed so much. It wasn't honest for him to stay here. Jack stood in the dark, and he felt his glass eye move a little in his face as the night wind passed. It was honest to do something else. He didn't want to acknowledge what he wanted to do now but descended the hill to its base in darkness without a light on. He checked his pockets and realised he'd brought his phone but decided he wouldn't turn on its torch anyway because that wouldn't feel right.

Coming down a little set of wooden stairs and off the hill, out onto the main road, he tasted the air and his forehead ached under the light of the lampposts. There were some muddy fields in front of him, some crops, he supposed. He turned and looked at the swirling haze of giant, dark trees on the hill his path had just broken out from. They all looked bigger in the night. He looked down the road and heard blaring speakers, saw a rainbow of neon that dazzled him and left him even more exhausted than before. He checked the address for Agatha's house on his phone and noticed a walk through the woods that he could take there. He asked himself why he couldn't just go back. Maybe Agatha would be there too. He could apologise for leaving her in the clinic. He would go back.

He descended another road with a battered walkway sign and the lead of a dog tied around a gate. He tried picking a berry from a bush, lowered it into his mouth, and realised too late that it was premature. He spat it out. His feet hurt slightly as he walked, so did his back. The path reminded him of one that he had taken in Cornwall in his childhood, down towards a black roaring sea. He knew it was the same time of night as then—the exact same, without a minute's difference. It was the same moment. It was a moment chosen for him to return, if not to Agatha's house, then to the distant past, and ridiculously, perhaps, to a past life of his. Jack looked at his hands in the night and saw how pale and worn out they were and realised he had no trade and no skills but could have been rendered something in another world. Agatha, too, could have been; her mother, also. He walked in a straight line amongst curled brambles for what certainly felt longer than an hour.

Out of the lurching spikes and off the ancient path, which had been used by a man similar to him some five hundred years before, Jack stepped into the high street, he walked roads of screams, blaring lights, cars, faces and arms twitching with glee before bright rectangles and beheld the church, St Michael's, he had known in childhood. It had been years since he'd entered it. Many a time he had passed it but never entered—and yet it had always been here. Had it waited for this moment for all of Jack's years? Perhaps he had wanted to preserve his memory of the church, Jack wondered, and that's why it had taken him so long to return. He feared that entering it might reveal that it had undergone the same changes that everything else had and seeing it so altered would mean that there was truly nothing left of the old world, nothing unless he fought to save it himself. In avoiding the church, had he avoided that duty: to fight for the old world?

Jack craned his neck up into the dark. Stars were only apparent above the church because light pollution was so general everywhere else. He studied the church yet noticed that it oddly seemed embarrassed in the dark at its own still semi-luminous stones, that its tower crouched in the shadow of a giant oak. Jack stupidly asked himself why the church was embarrassed. Then he heard shouts. He turned and looked opposite and saw that the massive party with the blinding neon lights was going on in Agatha's house itself, the red *Barbiecore* light flaring from the window onto his cheeks. So this was it. The wind blew through the belfry of the church, and bats scattered behind him as he walked, the shouts within increasing into screams.

'Is this the fight for the old world?' Jack asked.

Again, there was that strange tablet of a door—tilted open this time. Jack approached, wondering if he'd be thrown out by the shaking, wide-eyed celebrants he had already glimpsed inside. One window was open to the left of the door, from which air seemed to be rapidly rushing out. He wondered whether there was a fire.

'WOOOOOOO.'

'Oooooooooooo.'

'—aaaaaaaaaaaaaaaaA!!'

This was the first proper party Jack had ever been to. The music was some combination of drill and dubstep. The speakers, wherever they were, seemed to shoot out sound over and over again like automatic rifles into the twitching bodies of the crowd. (Was this the heart of hell?) Here were the sufferers, the horrors. The front room was so filled with people that neither the ceiling nor the floor seemed unpopulated. Everything throbbed. The spaces between people evaporated and extended in mere moments. In one moment, Jack was standing in an empty corridor with a sky-blue wall at its end and a white stairway. In another, he was in the extremely tall Mrs Alice Darger's arms as she grabbed, and felt, and asked him who he was, and said he was cute, and kissed him with an open mouth on his forehead so hard that he was worried she had taken a bite out.

The main room encompassed the entirety of the house's downstairs floor except for the corridor. The cameras were still there. Jack looked and saw their little red lights and realised that they were also recording. There were three of them, and behind two of them stood a pair of bearded men with skin that looked dark as obsidian under the party lights. One of them still wore a balaclava, although the other one found it too hot to keep his on, and so he let it dangle around his neck like a second face. The ceiling throbbed with pain.

'AAAAAAAAAAAA.'

The women were all white but for one very confused-looking mixed-race girl. All of them drank and were continuously given more drinks from under the kitchen counter. The cameramen and the Southeast Asian men who gathered in the four corners of the room never drank. They seemed to entertain themselves with the antics that were in front of them, both hating and enjoying what they saw on display.

Jack nearly knocked the shot glass out of the hands of a man of his own size with streaks of green hair and bright, almost flashing blue eyes. He shouted a slur at Jack, but he couldn't hear it. The waves of sound shot down his spine and up into the space above his head, between it and the suddenly low ceiling. Clearly, most of these people were from a previous party, and Alice had lured them in for another one after they were thrown out of the pub. Jack looked and saw, standing in the middle of the room, another straggler, a young boy who had probably been just as curious as he was and had simply wandered in. The boy wasn't dancing. Like Jack, he wasn't dancing. He couldn't have been older than sixteen. And how old—the music shifted to pullulating synths—was Jack now?

He lurched to the corridor and saw somebody (Agatha?) running up the stairs. Then the crowd surged, and pressed, and kept him back in its huddled mass. It was a microorganism restraining an errant cell.

'aa-aaaaaaaaaaaaaaaaaaaaaaaa.'

What about the air? The scent was of human sweat, and the lights in it were furious. Again, he wondered, was there a fire? Fairy wands were passed out, and each time one of them was turned on near Jack's face, he wondered whether he was going to have a seizure, awaken the epilepsy that an unknown ancestor had cursed him with. The music switched to rap. The entire room tried to scream and shout without saying the word that would permit the men in the balaclavas to violently assault whoever it pleased them. How many degrees removed were they in this situation from some scene in Haiti or Rhodesia? The women churned. They shouted. They were tense. The men shuffled.

Jack started to jump up and down to create some space for himself, and the others mistook it for dancing. He worried that his glass eye would fall out. It would be shaken out of his head and trodden on and smashed up, exposing the hideous white swelling under it. He jumped up and down, and brushed against gibbering women and random clerks from Sainsbury's who were also there, and told himself it wouldn't happen, and it *did!* His eye fell out. It dropped like a tear from his face onto the ground, before being immediately shattered under the hoof—no, heel—of ... *Basil Alawi?*

Jack looked up from where he crouched on the ground and saw Basil smile, thought about tackling and battering him into submission. But Basil just smiled. And then the energy needed, the anguish required for violence, left Jack as he began to get up. It really was Basil! He was real. Jack was still much taller, but it seemed as if Basil had grown to the same extent Jack had shrunk, *and they looked eye to eye now?* The rap was still blaring, and yet the words that passed from Basil to Jack and from Jack to Basil were oddly, exceptionally clear. Basil wore a white eyepatch. Jack could hardly look at him with his own true, busted white eye.

'I am not going to be charged,' Basil said. 'You are going to be charged.'

Jack stared into the socket and watched the dark tongue cower in its cave.

He imagined himself saying: 'Am I going to jail?'

And Basil replied in real life, 'Yes, you are going to jail.'

And he imagined himself saying: 'So you are free?'

And Basil smiled in real life and said: 'Yes, I am free. Look around you. I am free.'

And Jack imagined that Basil himself was the chimera, was the ruler of Bothelford, and the dancing legions about him were his hypnotised slaves, his collaborators, and those it had persuaded to unwind (since long before he was born) everything good in England and the world. And where was Fahir? Perhaps it was true that Fahir was at the party too and that this would be the site of his arrest, that all he had been 'promised' by the officer partly responsible for his own blinded eyeball had been false. Maybe the gang still held all the power they had garnered or were permitted to secure from the beginning by the state, and Fauna's silly video —*like his own ridiculous attack on Basil*—had done nothing but to accelerate its growth. The dancers bobbed. The bandage-white face of Alice Darger wailed with an extraordinary joy.

Three of Basil's teeth glowed blue in the party lights: all fillings from surgery in his boyhood. His hair twirled at the ends into spires. A tail seemed to drop from behind his tailcoat. This time, he wore a bow tie that was so obnoxiously pink it made Jack feel sick. His face was the familiar obsidian of the cameramen. Whether Basil actually looked like this or simply appeared to do so in Jack's strange vision, Jack couldn't tell anymore. Jack's blue eye seemed to see Bothelford as it wanted to look. His white eye, he knew, saw it as it was or what was underneath it: the beast's domain. Jack didn't know what beast—but even stammering in front of Basil's masks and paraphernalia, that phrase, *the beast*, lodged in his throat.

'I am sorry that your mother couldn't make it.'

'Ooooooooooooooooooooooooooooooooooooooooooooooooo oooo.'

'—What?' said Jack.

Basil asked him if he wanted to have a fight, a proper fight, outside or even in the basement, where they could finally settle their differences, make up, and a tiny black boy with a balaclava on his face came over and gave something to Basil that looked like a cigar case and left with a plastic object under his hoodie. Jack told him no.

'If you don't,' Basil said, 'we are going to pay you a visit. Come *play*.'

Jack couldn't tell if Basil was drunk or simply empowered by the spirit of the evening. For some incomprehensible reason, Jack asked about Frederick Williams and if he was here, and Basil went on his phone and showed him a *BBC News* article about an applicant to Cambridge University arriving there on a summer school programme to study Chemistry and drinking a poison, killing himself. The cause reported was transphobia. Jack didn't know if it was Frederick. But he guessed that it was. He wept spontaneously.

Basil said, 'He was truly insane, and he was smart enough to realise that. Therefore, this is what he did.'

Jack's heart felt like it was beating inside his head.

'That's your friend,' Basil said. 'That is the friend that you chose over me, and so you see, you chose wrong, Jonathan.'

The thudding in his revolving brains was now as strong as the musical pulsing running through the room itself, and Jack wondered if the inside of this living-room-kitchen-dining-room stuffed with people who might as well be brain-meat corresponded exactly to what was biochemically going on inside his own skull. The white walls were skull. The stairs to the basement and the upstairs were the jaws. Outside was the world. *Outside was still the world!*

'I'm not Jonathan. My parents christened me Jack.'

'...?'

'I am going to take Agatha away from here, and there's nothing you can do about it, and I don't care if you're following me, Basil, or who will arrest me. Do you know why?'

The brief wince of pain that Basil felt from hearing Jack's voice horrifically slid from his face like the curtain over a corpse. Here was the full extent of the smiling void.

'*Because you love Agatha,*' Basil said, eagerly. '*And now she is the age of consent—a Western abstraction! —You feel free to pursue her just as I did when she wasn't in the past!!*'

Jack froze.

The screamers churned and lurched in the skull kitchen and inside his own skull.

'We are all men,' said Basil and patted Jack on the shoulder. 'It is only natural.'

('—Then I'm not a man,') Jack said, only to himself. ('I'm not a man.')

Basil compressed Jack's shoulder, and the crowd dissolved and let him lead Jack through to the corridor near the entrance. The stairs to the basement had smoke emanating from them. Jack wondered how truly cold they were to make them like that, only to see another man in a mask emerge up and out of the room below carrying a fog machine. This time, it was one of the drunk English partygoers with a makeshift ghost mask—which, bizarrely enough, he had either thought appropriate to bring with him or he had found in the basement in one of the bins of props that Alice Darger used in her videos. Basil stood right behind Jack.

'I have decided I am not to marry Agatha,' Basil said.

'I don't believe you,' said Jack.

'More—' Basil searched for the word. '—*around* ...'

Jack imagined everything that Bothelford had ever been, from its Pagan cave discovered near its mine to the strange inscriptions in St Michael's graveyard, from its ancestral farm-land to the cold steel mills of the nineteenth century, from its tiny, tribal pre-Roman wars to the gargantuan wealth of the British Empire, from the smog that it tasted during the Industrial Revolution to the familiar, scattered gore of Viking invasions, that everything dead, that everything came rush-ing—*now*—into his life, back. He was struck by lightning by these memories. For, in the other room, were the descendants of so many thousands of people, and so many thousands of them would either have no children after the end of this, his generation, or would simply cease to be English to such an extent that their own families would cease to recognise them. This was today. This was now. And now, in that other room, history was dying, heritage was dying; custom sprawled out her arms and exposed her breasts, afraid simultaneously of the death that was coming and paralysed by her own deliberate ignorance of it. They were all going.

Jack, too, was one of these. For Jack, too, was going. He was worn away and would indeed go down and be stabbed by Basil in the back of the neck. It was logical and increasingly common here ... *wherever this was*, this old house that might have creaked with old spirits but ten years ago. But now those spirits were dead too! For whom did they have to embarrass with their hauntings, now that Basil was here, and the boy in the mask had a knife—Jack was sure—and Jack himself was destined to go down the stairs and bleed and bleed out? It was all very simple, really, for this was the end of England. Of him. In another age—*but this wasn't another age, this was the end!*

'Do not go up the stairs,' said Basil.

'DO NOT GO UP THE STAIRS,' the chimera screamed.

But Jack ran up the stairs for his dear life, even though it was the end. And even though it was the end, he found Agatha silently sitting in her bedroom on the left, the door of which was labelled with a list of names—('A queue!' thought Jack)— and saw such a smile on her face when he retrieved her that he too wondered if he were in love. She wore a jumper and a skirt that were too big for her and had clashing horizontal and vertical stripes. There were unwrapped presents on her bed that were decorated with spots and ribbons. There was a can of mace by her little mirror. ('Is this her birthday party?')

'*Come back down here!* NOW,' screamed Basil.

But Basil's screams fell on deaf ears. For they were going home, the English girl and the English boy, whatever was left of their home or wherever they could find one. Not here.

'Get Jessie,' Agatha said, passing into the corridor with Jack and opening the door on the right. But the room was empty. Monkey wallpaper dressed a wide window that directly viewed the sharp spire of St Michael's, which had gotten brighter? 'Not here today ... get Jessie tomorrow.' Agatha looked older, remarkably so. An old soul had taken possession of her. That, and more than a litre of alcohol.

Jack took Agatha's hand, and she let him hold it. Basil surged up the stairs. He rushed up at them, he came for them, and as he emerged, Jack saw there were party strings caught around his belt that might have looked like cobwebs downstairs. They hung oddly. Basil was furious, but as he passed under the light from above, the light illuminated the ridiculous thing that he actually was. Basil wore makeup, skin-lightener, too much. He was wearing white-face or on the verge of doing so. Basil's outfit, whatever material it was made of, was so ornate and elaborate that it had spiralled into the costume of a sheikh. He had started by imitating an Eton student with the coattails, before allowing layers of undershirts and overcoats to suffocate whatever he had in mind. He was not English in the slightest but an Ottoman bull clown imported for amusement. And though Basil screamed and sneered, he came to realise then, with Jack on his feet, however scared and blind the boy was, that Jack was strong—could smash his fist into his other eye, gore it before his faction stormed the stairs.

The church waited outside. Basil said nothing to Agatha; Agatha said nothing to Basil. This part of the house, this upstairs, was decorated nicely. Its carpets were a soft cyan. Its doors were white originals. There was a clean bathroom with only a few half-empty glasses on the side of its sink. As Jack passed down the stairs again with Agatha, he felt that this place perhaps represented Alice Darger's best-kept secret—that in spite of everything, and especially despite what this floor was seemingly used for—Alice had once loved her family, her husband, with whom she had first picked out this house sometime in the nineteen-nineties. Briefly, Jack wondered if that had been a time when the apocalypse of England was unimaginable. On one wall, Jack noticed an Oasis poster. Clearly, Alice Darger wanted to preserve the illusion that she was living in a better, purer time. But then they descended.

Basil promised he would see Jack again. But Jack knew he would never see him again unless it was at the end of a gun. He didn't mean to threaten Basil in thinking this, or maybe he did, but there was just no feasible way the two could ever encounter one another again without something like that happening. As Jack and Agatha reached the bottom of the stairs together, Jack told himself that he couldn't come back here either, because this house, this house right in the middle of England, was a house of lies. That is all that it was. It was a house of cowardice, Jack told himself, that entertained itself with pretty fantasies upstairs where it could still maintain its dignity but which downstairs was infiltrated with the most noticeable enemy the country had ever known. And maybe if he had read *Beowulf* at that time, Jack would have speculated that such a foe was more evident than the monster Grendel, who had marched from the fens on King Hrothgar some thousand and a half mythical years ago. But now was not the time for such thoughts. Jack knew they could neither stay here nor necessarily move to his house, half of which already belonged to foreigners, although one day he would be forced to reclaim it for the sake of his parents. He wanted them to live and die in the old world on the other side of this monstrosity, the modern one.

Perhaps Basil, as Jack and Agatha passed him, turned and yelled to Alice Darger, or any of the quiet men he seemed to know in the corners of the main room. Maybe he screamed, called for their blood. And yet he was drowned out. The noise was too loud, too maddened, dismal, terrifying, and exhausted, finally. Maybe Basil sighed into his own obsidian hands. For, in truth, Basil was not at home either, although he occupied the house, and perhaps he too assumed that he would one day leave it and leave England or be shut out of it, because that would be better than being killed in it by the mounting anger of locals like Jack.

The front door hung open like the grate of a crypt Jack couldn't tell if he was leaving or entering. Yet, without question, Jack led Agatha out into the dark. She took a plastic fairy wand to light the way out. It malfunctioned; she gripped it anyway. The air tasted clear.

'I'm sorry I didn't go in the clinic with you,' said Jack.

'It's OK,' said Agatha. 'You came back. Thank you for coming back.'

She kissed his ear; he didn't like that he liked it.

'Where to?' she said. Her face was angular, tense, and yet behind her usual pained features, there seemed to be a splendour that excited her. Jack held Agatha's hand and took her across the street as a few eyes from the front windows of the house followed them and Mrs Alice Darger screamed into herself like a firework bursting before it burns out. Yet they did not look back. They walked. They walked and walked.

They crossed the street, and Jack jammed his hands into the lichen-covered gates of St Michael's and pulled like he had never pulled before. The gates opened. How long had it been derelict, if it was derelict? The old still went here, but perhaps they locked it up during the week to prevent the young, or certain parts of the young, from getting into it and vandalising it for their cause. And yet they were in! Few who saw them were inclined to follow them in. It was too late. Those who watched stared as they saw the torn gate close behind Jack and Agatha, and the mark Jack had broken into the front of the gate looked like a smirk.

As for inside, it was very dark. No longer did Jack feel marooned inside the structure of his own head as in the Darger house, but neither did he feel alone with Agatha. There was something else in here, some presence. During the day, the church was just a church, but at night it was a colossus. The church interior was so large in comparison to the packed, tortuous maze they had just fled that its ceiling seemed broader than the sky they had walked under between the two zones. The church floors were chequered with black and white diamonds. The benches were arranged like pianos in an abandoned music shop, dusty and oblong and some of them collapsing or unbalanced, weakly hinged. The stained-glass window above everything was ignited by the lights of the town behind it, even the party lights, and the enormous figure of God's avenging angel surged before them, perhaps even out of the glass frames that bound him or merely held him back until the time was right. Doves descended from the roof of the church, and one of them made its nest in a box of children's playthings in the front area reserved for schoolchildren.

Hardly had Jack opened his mouth when he heard the echo of a strange fizzing noise. He turned and saw that Agatha had opened a rum-and-Coke can from her pocket. He felt like berating her briefly, but as she set the can down and started walking to the other end of the church—God's house, he remembered Oliver Turner calling it—he felt oddly compelled to follow her, to hear what she might have to say. Now that Agatha was sober enough for another drink, Jack considered, maybe she wouldn't slur her words as badly this time.

Through the other stained-glass window behind them, portraying scenes from Eden, the lights of the party flickered and changed to a dark, violent red. The red passed right into the centre of the church, falling not on Jack one bit but entirely behind the head of Agatha as she walked. The lights formed a surging, glowing nimbus behind her head: a red halo? Then she turned away from the end of the church, its font, and grinned strangely at a high illustration on the left side of the wall. It was the image of two gaunt figures, surrounded by a plethora of others, all nude, done up in very withered, very ancient paints.

'I don't know what that is,' said Jack.

'*I know what it is. That happens* ... at, like, the end of the world to the meek and the true, doesn't it? Have I gotten that wrong?'

An ancient vision echoed in Jack's head: what was the name of the lady he had seen in his dream again? Who was the girl, the elf, who had left him the twig? Why did he feel like he was before a figure from the beginning of England? And why was he thinking of this when he wasn't drinking, taking Cipralex, but sober and yet more grounded in the present than he had ever been?

'Seems about right,' said Jack. He distracted himself by look-ing back up at the figures on the wall again. It did look like they were being saved, in spite of it all. Perhaps it was because of all that had gone wrong that they had to be saved.

Agatha walked slowly down the aisle with her half-blinking fairy light, taking her steps very slowly and elegantly, and per-haps dreaming to herself of a future wedding in this very place after its restoration. Seeing her walk, Jack wanted *this*, whatever 'this' was, to last as long as it possibly could. He wanted one of her steps to last for one century and another to last another. If it would take a thousand years for him to wait in this safe haven before the Day of Wrath, or God's redemption of the meek, or whatever it was, then he was prepared to wait. He didn't really believe in God. But he was very happy to see Agatha being just a little at peace and felt pleased with his own courage to escape with her. And so, for a few minutes, they stayed.

It was, after all, a better option than simply returning, already, to the outside world—to that kingdom of death and lies that infiltrated everywhere, even here: there were Diver-sity Outreach posters by the church doors. Nevertheless, as Agatha reached the doors again, Jack decided he should follow her, and as she beckoned him, he wondered both where they would go and what they would have to do. Whether the police were following Jack and what Basil had said about his being charged were true or not, they decided together that they had to leave this terrible 'settlement', which did not have a name anymore and was not Bothelford. Holding hands, they walked for another hour, out of the church, farther into town, past more lurching partygoers, beyond the strangers selling drugs on the street corners, to get to the train station, to get on the very last train, to go ... where, they hadn't decided. Anywhere that wasn't here and wasn't becoming like here and could serve them as a home for long enough, that would be more than acceptable!

They were going. Yet as the plastic carriage doors closed behind them, and Jack happily discovered the train to be empty but for them, and a few men coming towards the station with heavy, dog-like faces, beards, and mouths clambered towards the doors and were shut out at the last minute, he remembered Jessie. Jack remembered they were leaving Jessie Waters. It, of course, wasn't just Jessie—but everyone in the town they knew and loved, that they were leaving. Doubtless, there were many hundreds, if not thousands, of children on the lists of the gang, on the *white tings* group chat. And what was leaving town with Agatha, at the end of the day, Jack concluded, but a terrible retreat? Where would they go? What would they do with themselves to live and work in the safer, and yet infinitely more expensive, place they were heading to? For that was becoming the luxury nowadays: to live in a town where your daughter, your sister, your friend could walk home safe. Was it even worth leaving, after all? Jack certainly couldn't afford anything better with his skills, which were as rudimentary as those of his entire generation. Their whole plan was a failure from the start. Nor was it even their plan: Jack had dragged her into this situation, like so many others, on the spur of the moment!

But then Agatha held his hand and told him that everything would be all right, and in the depths of his heart he knew it would be so: 'Don't worry. You can go to sleep now.' His mind drifted as she spoke. He drifted into thoughts that were ever so slightly above and below reason.

The gangs and the education system and the state responsible for aiding and abetting their havoc had destroyed Bothelford and had destroyed many an English town and city and soul; but in the process, they had also destroyed themselves. With the vanishing of types like Jack and Agatha into distant, ghostly parts of the country, the barbarians and their pathetic enablers would be left alone with each other and would soon be helpless. He felt and knew this. All the welfare used to sustain them would dry up like the thin stream Jack had encountered once in the far north that was utterly clogged with rubbish and had an Indian man washing his feet in it. The civilising process his own parents had used to keep their road clean would now be entirely abandoned; this general strategy was sensed amongst the English. It was more than known. Jack and Agatha would head farther into the country. They would exist again on the ancient laws of the land. He would be a lord and the keeper of a castle, or so he dreamed he would be, and refuse any engagement with society.

They would find the perfect spot for England to be reborn in, and it would be reborn through them, in particular. They would learn to grow tomatoes and strawberries and keep poultry and farm pigs, and theirs would be a hard life, but a true one, and all that they had would be theirs, and they would guard it well. Half-asleep in his chair in the midnight carriage, Jack dreamed of Agatha as a shieldmaiden and many hundreds of great ancestral ghosts and literary figures cheering them on, celebrating their return to the soil that had once nourished such strength in their own ancestors.

Then, before he fell entirely asleep, Jack compared the silliness of all he had just thought about to what once must have seemed the silliness of ministers importing tens of millions of foreigners into his country, foreigners who came from parts of the world that hated England more than anything. To the great lords and kings of the past, this would have sounded exactly as absurd, evil, and ill-judged as it really was. 'Then why', thought Jack, 'should the kind of world I want be imaginary? After all, the world we live in now was once nothing more than a madman's dream!'

The lights of the train carriage shunted over his eyes as it rushed, quickly, into the countryside—launched from tarmac, flew among wild grasses. Men boarded; men stared, and saw Agatha, and instantly sympathised. All knew. How can an Englishman look at someone like that without knowing? Never did they sit by her but honoured her quarters, the four seats she had saved for herself and her friend. Ultimately, the train itself was nothing less than a rocket fired long ago from the heart of Jack Grundon towards the outer limits of a new world. He talked in his sleep sometimes about the end of this one, this world. Some strangers laughed, but the English, increasingly, did not. Eventually, the train carriage emptied out again. The men went on their way.

In the meantime, Agatha laughed as Jack started snoring once more, and the light of the splendid old sun flecked through the entire carriage as hundreds of birds—somewhere—started to sing. Her own wings extended. Jack didn't see or know then what this meant, but she smiled on him with the eyes of Marine Emery—a spirit reunited with her friend from a time before Bothelford was gone.